Degrees in Love

This book addresses
class & Race
discomforts
in interracial
Relationships

Degrees in Love

Tavi Wayne

TULE
PUBLISHING

Chapter One

"PARDON ME, EXCUSE me." Laney Travers's coffee was sloshing around in her WYQT travel mug, with dark brown streams beginning to emerge along the rim. "Could I just get past you? Thanks," Laney whispered as she squeezed herself past the two men sitting at the end of the row.

She was in such a hurry to be seated she didn't even have time to engage in her momentary worry about whether it was less offensive to have her butt versus her groin in people's faces, since obviously no woman except an early '90s Kate Moss could proceed any way but sideways.

She'd arrived at the Radisson Hotel a little later than she'd hoped.

Why did people refuse to leave the empty seats on the end when an event was bound to be sold out or standing room only? Or why couldn't they just offer to move down? There were at least fifty people in the room waiting for radio host Tie Stevens to speak. She had raced downtown from campus to see the National Public Radio program host and to have him sign her book. Laney willed her bags to be as quiet as possible, willed her coffee to calm down for a moment longer. After placing her mug on the floor, she glanced at the front of the room and took a quick breath in, heart pounding. Tie was staring directly at her... and was that a flicker of amusement that crossed his face?

Laney looked down, feeling her ears and cheeks warming. A moment later, she tentatively lifted her head.

Tie was now focused on Cheryl Wallace, the general manager of WYQT, the local NPR member station. She was expansively singing Tie's praises, reminding the audience of his publications as well as his best-selling book, *Everyone's Business*.

Ah! Her pen and notepad, of course. That was what she had meant to grab before Tie's brilliant green eyes had trapped her midmove. She rustled among the contents of her laptop bag and located her notebook du jour, found a blank page, tapped the pen that she was wise enough to tuck into the spiral binder, and finally felt settled.

Though what she could possibly have to write about Tie's anecdotes from his book... was virtually nothing. Still, one never knew. And she could doodle. Maybe starting with those beautiful eyes of his. Although a black pen would do nothing toward capturing the sparkle and glorious green hue of his eyes.

Laney tapped her pen on paper, ignoring the sideways glance of the irritating man sitting next to her. If he didn't want to deal with her, he should have moved his ass down. *Next to this nice mellow lady to my right.* Who seemed to be on Valium or Xanax. It was definitely a too-much-Xanax smile. She'd seen it on her sister Lola's face many times.

People began to shift in their conference room seats.

The station manager was finally closing. "That it's my

great pleasure to welcome to our studios well-known author and radio personality, host of NPR's *Biz-E Life* evening business program, Tie Stevens!" Ms. Wallace clapped enthusiastically and waited for Tie to shake her hand before she finally joined others, including *Biz-E Life*'s staff, in the front row.

"Hi, everybody." He had a shining white smile, and his greeting was even more enticing in person than it was on the radio.

Laney looked around. Was she the only attendee who found sexual intrigue in the voice of an NPR program host? Looking at him now... well, she couldn't imagine any warm-blooded creature *not* finding intrigue.

"Not to stand here conjecturing on how the economy will withstand the latest political debacle, or what small business owners should be looking for in the next election cycle," Tie was saying. "No, I promise none of that. I'm here to give you a little glimpse of the scenes behind *Biz-E Life* and some general observations from my book. And then I'll basically open it up to questions. As you can see..." He rounded the table away from the podium, and leaned back against the desk, half-sitting, half-standing. "I'm pretty laidback."

Just like his sultry voice. The authoritative voice that came into her home every evening at six thirty. The voice that conveyed such accessible business and economic information Laney actually felt confident enough to weigh in on her colleagues' occasional discussions of such matters. Who would have thought she, who dropped her economics class in college because her head swam, would have the nerve to casually opine on stocks? Tie's engaging program had even inspired her to subscribe to *Businessweek* and *The Economist*. He really seemed down-to-earth, seemed to "get" her. Well, his audience. Tie didn't know her—the connection she felt to him was a function of good radio.

And despite being a down-to-earth guy on public radio, Tie could pass for a celebrity anywhere. He was simply gorgeous, with his thick, golden-brown hair and enticing lips. What the hell was he doing in a radio studio? At least put the guy in front of the CPB/PBS cameras!

She was in awe, conscious of his attractive mouth, but in her own world, so she was startled when he once again caught her off guard—this time worse than before. He was looking directly at her, less amused this time but rather curious, expectant. Everyone turned in her direction during the pause.

Laney dropped her pen. "I'm sorry, I missed that. Excuse me?" She heard the man beside her take in and let out a long exasperated breath. If Laney weren't so mortified and distracted by Tie, she would have had a few colorful words for this man.

Tie grinned, a slight dimple forming in his right cheek, a dimple that complemented the slight cleft in his chin. Damn! He was hot.

He shook his head, a lock of hair falling near his fore-head. "I didn't say anything. You just looked like you *really* had something you wanted to share with me, or to ask."

Laney had no doubt that her normally tawny skin was

reddening. Tie might have noticed, because he quickly turned attention back to himself. "See, that's why I'm not Professor Stevens. It was clear from day one that I wouldn't have a clue how to manage a classroom!" The audience politely laughed, and Laney was, hopefully, forgotten.

She bent to pick up her pen. Could she do anything adult-ish without spacing out in the process? She hadn't been a twenty-something for a good while. How could she not notice that she was practically serenading the speaker with her eyes? No wonder he was distracted. So, she sat very still, looking up only to glance at the pastel-colored walls. Otherwise, she focused on creating small doodles—hearts for some reason—and tried not to look at the speaker.

Applause signaled the end of the session, and after the station manager jumped up to make sure that people wouldn't leave before a couple of "important" WYQT announcements, people patiently waited to file out of the room. Some made a point to move near Tie so that they could shake his hand, and those with a copy of his book had the natural excuse to ask for the favor of his signature.

As Laney passed Tie, she noted in her periphery that he appeared to face her. She tentatively turned his way. She wasn't distracting him right now, right? Laney continued to move along with the line, eerily aware that Tie's eyes were following her as he multitasked. She confirmed it by looking back once or twice. Suddenly, she turned around, drawn in his direction. Her knees weakened, so she steadied herself before trying to casually stroll toward him. There weren't many people left in the room at this point.

He looked at her expectantly. Laney couldn't figure out whether he seemed unsurprised to see her or again just fascinated and curious about her presence. "About earlier…"

"Yes? You did have a question?"

"No. Well, at least not one that was yet formulated."

"Ah," Tie said. "See, a professor would know how to read students' faces. I'm sorry."

"It's okay. I'm sorry I threw you."

"So is your question yet formulated?" He was rubbing the bottom of his lower lip.

His gaze on her was interesting. There was no sign of arrogance, no sign of impatience, no sign of anything but—could it be—something bordering on enchantment.

He smelled lovely. Not as though he wore a certain cologne but rather "Essence of Tie." She suddenly wished the room were completely empty so she could rest her head against his crisp white shirt, take in his scent, and get a break from those intense, beautiful eyes. Even through his clothes, she could tell that he had a hard, protective chest.

Instead, Laney sighed, shoulders dropping. "No. No, I'm sorry, Mr. Stevens—"

"Tie."

"Tie. I'm not sure why I felt the need to speak to you." She felt her face warming. "It takes a while for my thoughts to come together sometimes. Although, believe it or not, I'm the professor here. Maybe my intention was just to come and apologize for the disruption."

"No worries. Again, that was at least as much on me. My father is the professor in my family. His son went into 'show biz,' according to him," Tie said. "Where would we be if Einstein was rushed into articulating his questions, right? He asked the key questions—and, boy, were they key—when he was good and ready."

"Oh, Einstein. No pressure there."

Tie smiled. He just stared at her instead of giving her a friendly "bye." Laney tried to meet his gaze, as she wanted to appear confident, but she caught herself shifting her weight from foot to foot. Making matters worse, Ms. Wallace was standing nearby, with other staff. Though they busied themselves with talking, they were also obviously waiting to talk to Tie about their next moves, probably dinner or something. Laney gave the general manager credit for not just interrupting.

"Here I am taking up all your time, and I'm sure your producers…" Her voice trailed off.

He was still staring at her.

"You're really breathtaking. Stunning."

Laney looked at her feet, toward the station staff, toward the disappearing line, anywhere but back at his long, dark lashes. Her stomach fluttered and she was flooded with desire she had no idea what to do with. Her desire to kiss him suddenly became very urgent.

"I'm sorry." Tie's tone changed, his volume increased, he seemed to snap out of his trance, or whatever it was, and Laney's train of thought was disrupted. "I've held you up and I'm embarrassing you. I'm just used to speaking the truth, telling it like it is. Your presence—you keep stopping me in my tracks."

"Telling it like it is!" Ms. Wallace cheered, repeating Tie's tagline.

Laney found it hard to talk. "It's okay," she mouthed to Tie. He winked, showed his right dimple, then began to move toward Cheryl.

Laney turned toward the door in a daze, hoping she'd be able to remember where she parked the car. Wait! She didn't get her own copy of Tie's book signed! That must have been somewhere in her frazzled mind when she approached Tie in the first place. Her cheeks burned. Should she turn back this late in the game? Well, she couldn't make her impression on him any worse, right?

She hurried over to Tie, who had just rejoined the staff. "Uh, excuse me, Mr—Tie. I completely forgot I'd wanted you to sign my copy. I'm *so* sorry to bother you yet again. Could you…"

"Sign it for you? Of course." He returned to the table where he had been signing books. "To whom should I make this out?" He glanced at Laney with a—she was afraid to admit it, but it looked awfully seductive—look in his sparkling peridot eyes.

"Um, Elaine Travers. Well, Laney. Just Laney, please."

"Okay, just Laney, then." He was scribbling furiously. What on earth was he writing? Her name wasn't that long.

"Pleasure chatting with you for a moment, Laney." His gaze on her lingered, and as he handed the book back to her, his fingertips grazed hers.

She was immediately flooded with a tingly warmth and lightness.

"Pleasure is mine, Tie." *You have no idea.*

Not until she was outside in the sultry August air did she open the book.

To Laney, whose beauty leaves even me at a loss for words! If you have a moment, call me at 312-555-2753. Perhaps we can grab lunch or dinner. I'm in town only for a couple of days and I'd love to see your exquisite smile again.

Two pages of Tie Stevens's handwriting! Never mind how large the lettering. Never mind what it *said*. Laney's head felt light.

She caught a glimpse of herself reflected in the tall hotel window. What on earth did he find so stunning? Granted, he wasn't the first to comment on her looks, but with a face and body like his, and his fame... and she certainly wasn't looking her best, having come directly from a day of meetings on campus. She rustled her long, full, dark brown ringlets and, though she couldn't see them well in the dark reflection, she imagined her large, shining chocolate-brown eyes in her golden-brown, heart-shaped face staring back at her.

"Well..." She ignored the curious glances of people walking past. "You must have done something right this morning, chick." She smiled and made a mental note to thank Nette for talking her into wearing something, even just lip gloss, whenever she left the house. A mood boost, Nette had said.

Well, multiple compliments and an invitation to dinner

from Tie Stevens was about the biggest mood boost she could hope for.

But also the most intimidating.

Chapter Two

H<small>E REMOVED HIS</small> tie and ran his fingers through his waves. Thank goodness his executive producer, Blue, had joined him and the WYQT staff for dinner. Tie likely would have reflected poorly on the show if Blue had not been there to jump in with an engaging tale or two about going on air, going on assignment, or working with a particular guest. He had been so tired and preoccupied he couldn't track the conversation very well.

He kept thinking back to the brief encounter with the stunning woman he'd seen earlier that evening, after his talk. Luscious, dark locks, big, Bambi eyes, full lips, and skin that would melt in his mouth. Not to mention her very attractive figure. She'd been mesmerizing, first through her looks and then by her melodious voice. She must be one hell of a professor, with students hanging onto every word. A bit absent-minded, too, which somehow added to her charm.

It was a long shot, but hopefully she would give him a call and take him up on his offer to meet. He'd surprised himself by writing his phone number in her book. Usually, he was protective of his personal information.

He walked into the bathroom in his hotel room and glanced in the mirror. He did a double take as something occurred to him. He was White. She was Black. The bathroom lights were unflattering and made him seem paler than usual. Had she noticed? Did people still notice such things in more than a cursory way? Not that race was trivial, but it had no place in rules of attraction.

He was about to call his sister Meg but thought better of it, glancing at the bedside clock radio. It would be past her bedtime, and he had just video chatted with her yesterday. Instead, he dialed another number.

"Joe!" he said when the other end picked up.

"Hey, Tie. How'd the trip go?"

"Still here. It's going. Listen, I don't want to keep you, but about that contact information you promised me. I might as well try to squeeze myself onto someone's schedule while I'm here. I'm going to need a lot of money."

AFTER A FILLING Mediterranean lunch, Tie was doing research for his segment when his phone rang. It was an unfamiliar number, but he recognized the Columbus area code. Maybe…

"Hello, this is Tie Stevens."

"Hello, Tie Stevens." Yes! Laney. He recognized the quiver in her voice.

"Laney," he said, before she could introduce herself. "Good to hear from you!"

There was a pause. "Well, I found your… note… in the book you signed, and I thought I'd take you up on your offer. I'd love to meet with you over dinner."

He grinned, unable to help himself. "I'm really glad to hear that, Laney. I was hoping you'd call." He forgot about the task of reading notes. "How are you?"

"I'm good, thanks for asking. You?" The quiver in her voice was gone.

"Feeling great, now." He felt like a schoolboy—a giddy infatuation he hadn't felt in years. "So, what's good to eat around here?"

He hung up the phone with the grin still on his face. His friends usually described him as "collected." And he tended to agree. So why was he so exhilarated by the prospect of a date? He'd been on many before. It was not just her attractiveness. And he didn't know her personality, although their phone conversation had been easy and pleasant. Maybe it was that tingly warmth he felt when his hand had grazed hers the evening before.

He spun in his chair, tapped his blue Cross pen on the desk, and looked at the neatly packed bookshelves. She was a professor. Probably with a PhD. Like his father. Oh, god, he hoped *not* like his father. She was probably brilliant and would ask him all sorts of questions about his education, queries that Tie often tried to skirt. He could imagine the dinner going downhill as soon as he finally admitted that he'd dropped out of college.

Ungrateful. Disrespectful. Fool. Waste. Mistake. Regret. Scattered words from his old man's vitriolic response the day Tie dropped out of college in his junior year remained seared in his memory. Dropping out was just concrete confirmation of what his father already thought he knew. Tie was destined to be a failure, a disappointment.

It had been distressing enough to his father that Tie hadn't yet decided on a major, although he had taken a lot of business and communications classes. These weren't real areas of study, according to his father, whose ivory tower mentality shunned practical knowledge. Therefore, Tie could hardly hope to establish any kind of respected doctoral path with those foundations. But when Tie actually stopped attending classes, notified the registrar, and walked off the campus of the University of Wisconsin, Madison, without looking back, that was the final straw. Soon after, ties were all but severed between the two men, and Tie managed to build a new life for himself. And he was okay with it. Or so he usually thought.

But, what would Laney think about his background? Hopefully, it wouldn't come up. His lack of formal education was not widely known. He had mastered the ability to talk about his career path without mentioning his education, and hopefully that would suffice in this case. Let this intriguing woman know that he was worth her time.

He spun back to the desk and put his head in his hands. Why was he letting his father's condescending voice into his head again? Maybe she wouldn't judge him. After all, she had come to hear his talk and had actually bought the book. He must rate highly enough in her mind to warrant taking time out for that.

Still, his grin had faded and he looked at his notes without seeing them. This was why he ended up with women who were "safe." Women who wouldn't question his pedigree. Intelligent women, yes, but those who weren't concerned about titles. Laney would be his first doctoral-level date in years.

Just what sort of evening would tomorrow turn out to be?

Chapter Three

A DELICIOUS MEAL with a delicious man. Her fantasy lover. Was this for real?

But two days after she had found the courage to call Tie, her stomach was twisted in knots. How was she supposed to prepare for a date with him when she had no clue how to do so? It would be challenging enough with John Doe from Match.com… but this was Tie Stevens! The man whose voice alone, coming through the airwaves, never failed to leave her slightly moist between the legs. No man should have that much power.

Snap out of it, Laney. You're thirty-two years old. No man can render you powerless. Pssshhh. Plus, she had a valuable resource—her best friend, Nette.

"A GARBAGE MAN? As in waste management?" Because, really, they might not have been on the same page. She was sitting in a coffee shop later that afternoon with Nenette, as per their near-daily routine. She tried to patronize this shop just outside of campus as much as possible, because it was run by students. The workers took pride in claiming their commitment to sustainability and "eating locally."

Nette shook her angled, red-haired bob as she smacked her yellow "sugar" packet, one of many stocked in her purse. "I just don't know what other kind of garbage man there is, Laney. It's not some pretentious metaphor, if that's what you're asking." She brought the cup to her lips. The steam practically warped her facial features and, as usual—even while her thoughts were jostled by Nette's news—Laney wondered how the hell anyone could sip practically boiling liquid. But she also always wondered what it would be like to experiment with some of those extras—the creamer and the coffee varieties, and the fancier espresso-based drinks in just about every coffee shop these days. Black coffee just seemed neater and purer somehow. Although her palate often craved more.

"Okay, okay, but there's the guy that drives and the one that hangs off the back and actually collects all the trash."

"Sometimes they do both; it doesn't matter. But, yes, you could recognize him as the guy on the back; he's one who hangs from a moving vehicle. So what." She pretended to be disappointed by the "bitter" taste of the clearly saccharin coffee and shook another yellow packet. This was all part of the ritual, but every move seemed more pronounced, more emphatic this time. Maybe Laney was riling her best friend, but she couldn't let this go. How was one to deepen a friendship if major new information or inconsistencies appeared without any attempt at explanation?

"Nette! You're a germaphobe! This isn't exactly a nonissue. You have a hand sanitizer right by your front door, right here on this table, you take your own cutlery everywhere, and you *never* allow shoes to be worn in your condo. Indeed, sometimes they stay out of the house, no matter how new." She glanced at her three-month-old Danskos. "Last month you wouldn't have been able to *look* at a garbage truck without taking out your hand sanitizer."

"It's because of fear of contagion. All that is true, except—and I'll say this only once more, my intellectual friend—it's called mysophobia. Real condition, not to be made fun of any more than your ADHD."

"I know that. But surely you get why I'm astonished. You could barely look at a man collecting garbage before but now you're literally seeing one." She clapped her hands for emphasis. "And I'll say *this* only once more. Stop diagnosing me with ADHD."

"Anyway, he's hot as *hell*. One impulse is overriding the other at present. One obsession suffocating the other. We just happened to cross paths one morning. I was hooked; he was hooked, so I put his number in my phone. This could actually be therapeutic."

Laney thought about that while her own coffee was cooling down. "I guess you're right." But Nette's crisp way of speaking was annoying, especially at times like this, when her other friends would probably be gushing. "So, you've even thought about, like, letting him into your fresh linens?"

This time Nette looked directly at her, her gray eyes locked in so Laney couldn't have glanced away even if she'd wanted to. "Yes. I was even able to do that, but not without discomfort. We've been fucking in his bed. And his couch.

And even his kitchen table, which we've also eaten on since. So there we have it. Hard. And soft."

"The surfaces or the—"

"Both. I think I love him, actually," she said, barely audible, as she wrinkled her small, lightly freckled nose.

Laney let her words float into her ears and in the space between them. She couldn't think of a single thing to say. It made sense, perhaps. If she was going to get "dirty," she might as well defile every previous sacred surface in an enjoyable, safe way. Her friend was an enigma sometimes but usually quite logical. Although she suspected that the whole "arrangement" occurred in a much more ironic and fortuitous way than Nette led on. She was no more invulnerable than the next woman.

Laney's palms sweated and her heart raced just thinking about Tie, and how he was consuming her thoughts lately. And how, hypocritically, she had yet to even mention her encounter with him, not to mention the planned date, to Nette.

As if Nette were tuning in to Laney's unspoken words, she stirred her coffee redundantly and pointed the stirrer at her. "All these questions. To distract me from your story?"

Laney felt her eyes widening. "What story? I'm not trying to distract you. For heaven's sake, you just told me that you're in love with a trash man! I'd hope that you would be startled if I changed the subject after you telling me something so huge!"

"We-e-e-ll, I'm inviting you to. Telling you to, actually. So spill it."

"Nette, come on. Who's the real table turner here? Don't drop hot info if you don't care for the follow-up. Not cool." She was avoiding her eyes.

"Spill it, Elaine."

Laney's sudden silence would be giving her away, but she had to take a few seconds to consider whether she was too irritated to share her thrilling new information with her closest friend and whether she would be able to tolerate whatever terse, judgmental crisp response she might have in return.

This was the same woman who, when they first met in college, scoffed, "I've never met a Black Elaine before. Elaine's not really a Black name."

Laney replied, "Have you ever met anyone named Elaine before?"

Silence. "Okay, maybe I'm just thinking of Seinfeld, which was a very, very White show."

"Mmm-hmm. By that logic, no Black woman should be named Phoebe, Rachel, or Monica, either. I should point out that I've actually never met a White Nenette before, by the way."

It was a wonder they had become best friends. Yes, Laney could hold her own around her. After all, there wasn't a damn thing to be ashamed of. And she needed her advice!

She took a deep breath. "We-e-ell, I've just started dating a celebrity."

Nette actually paused her ritual, set her coffee down, clasped both hands in front of her, and leaned forward. "A celebrity? You're a true academic, not just a part-time business instructor like me, so your definition of celebrity might be different from mine. Who is this celebrity?"

Well, when she put it like that… "Okay, maybe not a celebrity, although he certainly had a good turnout the other night when I attended his talk."

Nette slammed her hands on the table and leaned back, taking her coffee with her. "A talk. I knew it was another egghead or somebody like. One of those public intellectuals?"

"No, smart-ass. An actual media celebrity. Okay, NPR media, but still, heard by many, many, many people across the nation. Not just in Columbus and 'the surrounding areas.' It's like denying that Big Bird or Cookie Monster are child celebrities. PBS is equivalent to NPR, after all."

"Okay, enough with the public media campaign." She waved her hand. "Slide over the deets. Show me his pic, tell me whether you already got you some—those are the things Nette needs to hear." She sipped her coffee, its steam having thinned out a bit.

"First of all, there aren't any 'deets' yet. I mean I just met him. Thirty minutes, tops, including the phone call."

"So you haven't had your first date yet."

"That's kind of what I wanted to talk to you about, if you'll cool it with the thirst for rich gossip." Her eyes slid over Nette's face as she picked up her phone. "Here." She typed in the home page and there was Tie's handsome face, showcasing his beautiful smile and eyes, though the photo didn't begin to do him justice. "This is him. His name is Tie Stevens, and he's the host of *Biz-E Life*, NPR's evening business program."

"I know that much—I do listen to that show. But hot *damn* I had no clue Tie was so fine! Go, Laney!" She high-fived Laney and the latter basked in the glory. "Go figure. As usual, you got a fine catch."

"Okay," Laney said cautiously, after a big gulp of coffee. "With him and me in mind, I need you to help me to, you know, make a lasting impression on him."

"What do you mean?"

"This is like a fairy tale for me, Nette. A dream I've never dared to dream but which has nevertheless come true! And I don't want to spoil it. So you have to help me to look like, I guess *metaphorically*, a princess." This last part she whispered, embarrassed as hell. But she meant it.

"What? You're disgustingly gorgeous already. I've asked to borrow your eyelashes and cheekbones like a thousand times. What are you looking to do? You know you don't go changing for any man!"

Laney seethed. "This isn't just any man. He's a prince," she whispered. "Metaphorically."

Her bestie shook her head and put her hands to her temples. "Okay, I don't get where any of this is coming from, talk of knights on white horses and castles."

"I never said—"

"And living happily ever after… talk about putting the cart before the horse!"

Laney stared at her coffee. "There's another thing." She drew in a long breath. "He's White."

Nette's mouth hung open. "I can see that. And?"

"Well, I've never really dated a White man before because there is so much drama that comes along with it. In fantasyland, it's different. But in real life there's, you know, jungle fever and all that. But this is Tie Stevens! Never mind."

Nette's eyebrow was raised. Her friend couldn't possibly understand this subject.

"Really, not the point." She waved away Laney's concerns with her hand. "You've come for Nette's help, and I won't fail you. Shall we go to your house?"

"Okay, yeah, I guess that makes sense." She took a deep breath. "Okay. *Now* can we please get back to your guy? You haven't even told me his name!"

Nette settled probing eyes on her for a few seconds. "Devin. If we must."

Laney smiled, sitting back comfortably with her coffee.

AN HOUR LATER they were standing in Laney's bedroom. She'd brought up a bottle of wine and two glasses from her antique wine rack, an attempt to steady her nerves.

Nette stood at the doorway to her closet. "Wow. I haven't actually seen this space since before you moved in. It's so well-organized."

"Come on. You've seen my closet a million times. You always ask to borrow one of my scarves." She had colorful Indian scarves draped on one of the hanging rods. She was proud of her well-organized closet. It somewhat compensated for areas in which her organization was lacking, like her mind.

"I could swear every time I've been over, your closet door's been closed, and your nice little over-the-door shoe and purse rack are all that's in view. Wow, those are gorgeous scarves. I might have to borrow one."

Laney rolled her eyes. "So, give me a starting clue here. Narrow me down, what should I aim for?"

"Okay, okay, Nette's got you."

An hour and a half later Laney had an outfit laid across her bed—a bateau neckline, knee-length black dress that draped a little in the back, and displayed her curves just enough. On the floor next to her bed were a pair of never-worn three-inch heels with a sexy cutout. "There's a reason I haven't worn them," Laney protested.

It had been a decade since she forced herself into heels, and she didn't have pleasant memories associated with those slutty stilts. Dance music and men's wolf whistles echoed in her head and wrapped around the shiny pole she envisioned in the middle of it all.

"And there's a reason you haven't taken them back," Nette answered, bringing Laney back to the present. She shoved them on Laney's feet and ordered her to look at their sexy reflection in her full-length standing mirror. "And since you refuse to wear sandals, despite that your feet are like veal, you had better show off those glorious feet and legs however you can." Which had also meant no pantyhose and a direct order to shave.

A delicate, short crystal chandelier necklace lay alongside

the dress, accompanied by dainty hanging crystal earrings. "Just a little sparkle, to make you stand out in the night— especially since you're wearing black," Nette explained.

Finally, a matching lace bra and panty set, red and black, was neatly packed beside the dress.

"Makes you feel sexy. And, you just never know. What's the harm?" Nette winked.

Laney had to admit the outfit seemed promising, especially on her maroon-and-white duvet as a background.

Nette also had marched right out to her car when she saw the slim pickings in Laney's makeup "collection." Fortunately, she transported a fully stocked makeup kit wherever she went because "you never know."

Laney *thought* the woman in the mirror at her vanity could be her. There was a resemblance. But the intense colors and drama caught her off guard. She had to admit, the makeover complemented her features, and if she were going into a beauty pageant this would be the way to go, but she wanted to feel like herself with Tie, not some beauty pageant contestant he suddenly got in the bargain.

Nette read Laney's expression in the mirror. "You don't like it."

"Oh, I like it. You're really talented. You've done a terrific job at highlighting my features. Just look at my cheekbones! But, well, I guess I wear my colors more in my personality and clothing than on my face?"

Nette nodded slowly. "That you do." She sighed. "So the wannabe princess doesn't want to be too princessy. You're lucky I love you." She picked up a sponge and some makeup remover. "You might as well refill our wineglasses, though this won't take too long. Can we still go bold with the lip color?" Her eyes pleaded in the mirror.

Laney smiled and nodded.

"Great. And we'll just tone down the colors elsewhere."

"Yes, please." Laney poured them both more dry riesling. "I'd been meaning to talk to you about blush, actually…"

Fifteen minutes later, Nette asked, "So, feel like a princess now?"

"Yes, though not so much like a feminist. Thanks, Nette." Laney drew her into a quick hug.

Nette moved a lock of hair out of her friend's face. They had decided to keep things casual by letting Laney's long hair hang loose, though pretty clips just behind her temples allowed a few tendrils to strategically frame her face.

"But, as far as your fairy tale, Gloria Steinem, remember this. Your happily ever after is like Dorothy's shoes. In here." She pointed to Laney's head. "Here." She pointed to Laney's heart. "And here." She poked at Laney's abdomen.

"Mmm-hmm, I get the heart, and brain, but what the hell is this?" She circled her abdominal area.

"Courage. Your ovaries. I don't like to say balls, because we just don't have them. But you know what I mean. You have to take risks." She winked. "Always has been the case. Tie might or might not be a part of that happily ever, sweetie, but you're a gem, and you do deserve a happily ever after. Give it to yourself, babe."

"Oh, Nette." Laney's eyes moistened. Her friend's compassion and sweetness was a side Laney rarely saw. "Two highly educated women talking fairy tales. Who knew?"

"That said." Nette returned to her normal sharp tone. "Please assume the attitude that goes along with your makeover. Like, you're the shit, okay?"

"One hundred percent."

"Damsel in distress in not part of the narrative. At. All. Let me know how it goes, girl. Which reminds me." She went to her purse and pulled out a condom. She laid it by the lingerie. Then, after a moment of thought, she pulled out a few more. "You never know. And you owe me deets next time around."

"I guess I do." Laney sighed, closing the door behind her.

That was assuming that there would be any deets to pass along.

IT WAS JUST after six thirty. She had to get moving. She turned on the radio.

"Businesses ushering in Halloween an average of three days earlier than this time last year, overlapping with back-to-school marketing. So, be careful not to accidentally send your little one off to school in a witch's costume. Good evening, everybody! Welcome to Biz-E Life! *Coming to you live from Columbus, at our sister station, WYQT. I hear Northwestern fans aren't quite welcome here. I'll be back at our home station tomorrow. On to the business news…"*

Jay-Z's "Hard Knock Life" briefly played as an intro, and Laney smiled, though she knew it didn't bode well for the stock market.

Her pupils dilated and her heart sped up as soon as she heard Tie's voice. His sigh alone made her insides play pinball, and though she'd read somewhere—or maybe even heard on NPR—that one can't really blush in solitude, sometimes her cheeks warmed as if Tie were sitting next to her, gazing at her while serenading her with business news. These were her usual reactions, though certainly more intense now that they'd met. It was a wonder she managed to hear any of the news being reported.

After she got into her dress and touched up her hair and makeup, she was pushing it in terms of time, given the drive from Sheffield's campus, on which she practically lived, to downtown. She hadn't thought the details through. But she'd make it work.

Indeed, an hour later she was seated across from Tie at Sushi House, which overlooked the Scioto River. She smiled shyly at him in between studying menu items, as if she didn't know exactly what she'd be having. He'd put his menu aside nearly immediately and was unabashedly staring at her. Laney didn't ordinarily consider herself to be shy, but the intensity of his gaze was something to be reckoned with. She finally decided—she'd stick to her usual plan of a spicy tuna roll, unagi, and various other familiar pieces of sashimi—and focused on the sunset-illuminated water.

"Beautiful, isn't it?" she asked absentmindedly.

"She is, very much so." Tie's deep response caught her off guard and she turned her warming face toward him.

"I meant the water, of course. But thank you." She fiddled with her chopsticks.

"That's beautiful, too. It's not Lake Michigan, but I just love water." He leaned forward. "You mentioned that you're a professor. Where do you teach?"

"Sheffield College, right outside of the city."

"Oh…" The lines in his forehead deepened.

"Right, it's a small school. You likely wouldn't have heard of it unless you were from the area."

"Do you like it there?"

"Well, I'm up for tenure, so I'd better either come to love it or say good riddance!"

He brightened. "That's great! Best of luck to you. What do you teach?"

"Psychology."

"How's that?"

"Teaching? I love it. It's like I feel in total control when I'm in front of a classroom, while at the same time something else seems to be taking over me, channeling through me. I know that sounds contradictory. I can't explain it."

"I think I know what you mean. I'm in flow when I'm on air. Completely absorbed in the moment, riding the momentum seamlessly."

"Yes! Like that."

"And you do research?"

"Yes." Laney looked down and smoothed the napkin in her lap. "Childhood loneliness." She rested her gaze on his face again. "But let's not talk about it. It's a depressing subject, though very important."

Tie nodded. His eyes were spectacular, reflecting the

light at various angles, like gems. Her breath caught in her throat and her heart skipped a beat.

There was a momentary silence, but neither of them looked away.

"I'm very curious about how you ended up in the studio hosting my favorite public radio program." She smiled—seductively, she hoped.

Tie grinned and his pretty white teeth sent shivers down Laney's spine. "Aw, shucks. Your favorite? I'm honored. Let's see. My father always had NPR on, so I kinda grew up with it. The stories fascinated me. And you didn't have to sit in one place to get the full benefit, like you do with TV. Anyway, the short version is that I worked my way up from being an intern when I was in col—college. One of the internship locations is in Chicago, fortunately—that's where my home was.

"After that I just felt at home in the stations—in just about any role they stuck me in. The station manager of WLAK at the time, where I eventually landed, was impressed with what he saw in me, I guess, and I started doing some of the more substantive research and began to go on air for minor reporting. Um... sort of just climbed from there. Then, after many years, when they needed someone to replace Brent Rivers on the evening business program, look who was available."

Laney waved her hand in his direction, dismissing his nonchalant report. "Come on, I'm sure it wasn't just your availability. Don't be modest."

"No, seriously." He shrugged. "I was just well read on

the topics, had balanced views, and, I guess, they thought I had an engaging voice."

"That you do." *More like the sexiest voice on earth.* Who else could come across as sweet, sexy, funny, and authoritative at the same time? The man worked vocal magic. "So what does one study to become a radio host? At least, an NPR radio host. Communications?"

Laney couldn't be sure, but Tie's eyes seemed to momentarily dim, and he briefly looked away. "Yeah, communications, journalism, you know, then whatever specialization."

"Oh, like Click and Clack from *Car Talk*, MIT trained." Laney laughed. "So where did you do your undergrad?"

Another brief glance away. Maybe it was what her friends called her "psychology eye," but Laney's antennae began to go up a little. She wasn't boring him, was she?

His bright eyes landed on hers again, and she was relieved. "University of Wisconsin, Madison."

"Oh, good school. The Badgers."

Tie seemed to consider something, then smiled. "Yes, the Badgers."

"How about grad school? Any graduate work?"

"Nope, nope." He looked at her with a faint smile but failed to elaborate.

Not that it mattered much. "Well, in any case, I'm impressed."

Tie looked surprised. Then he chuckled. "Well, I'm lucky, I guess."

"And you have talent. You're smart as a whip. And funny."

Tie seemed to study her for a moment. "Thanks," he said quietly. Then, more loudly, enthusiastically, he added, "But somehow the conversation turned to me. Let's get back to talking about you…"

The waiter came by to take their orders. They decided to go full-on festive with sake.

Laney hadn't anticipated the long, lingering dinner between the two of them. Who knew they would have so much to talk about? Books, indie movies, favorite quotes, urban murals, and behavioral economics among countless other subjects. And he'd had such fascinating experiences. Such easy conversation led to a late evening. Late enough she was feeling quite giddy from all the wine by the time they decided to leave.

As they stood, Tie took her hand and led her out of the restaurant. His hand holding hers was the most sensuality she'd experienced in months. His touch put her in full throttle, and she felt the blood rush to her pelvis.

"I really enjoyed my time with you, Laney. Like, immensely," he said as they stood by her car.

"I had fun, too, Tie. So, where to from here, hottie?" She put her hand on his chest, suggestively, and marveled at her boldness. That was the sake in action.

"Well, I'm not ready for this evening to end. Especially with my leaving town tomorrow."

His words sobered her a bit. She'd known he'd be leaving soon, but tomorrow seemed a minute away.

She didn't know whether it was the sadness behind her

pouting or the action of her plump lips, but he moved in, tipped her head up by her chin, and planted the softest of kisses on her mouth. He paused. She didn't move. He kissed her a little more aggressively, allowing her a small taste of him. Her arms flew around his neck and she pulled his head even closer.

"God, this is perfect, Laney," he murmured between kisses.

She moaned in response, and they pulled impossibly closer together, so she was able to feel his welcome hardness on her belly. That was a wrap. Her body was weak with desire for him and she didn't have the motivation to fight it.

But she weakly nudged him away, trying to gain a little space time for her thoughts. She was free-falling. With the huge head start she had during her daily fantasies about him through the airwaves, this moment was inevitable now that they'd met in person. But he'd be gone tomorrow. They would have a fleeting experience that might eventually be indistinguishable from fantasy. What would that be like for her?

"Um, so, we could go to a nightclub. Believe it or not, I do occasionally get out, and I know a couple of okay spots around here." Her voice was breathy and shaky. She didn't sound convincing.

He seemed to still be recovering from the kiss. "Okay spots? That's not a hard sell, is it?" His chest was heaving as he looked around.

But Laney had already seen his true desire in his darkening eyes. "Well, we could walk off dinner..." His eyes returned to hers, and they seemed smokier than ever, his lips fuller.

"But there are other ways of working off dinner." He bent down and kissed her shoulder and neck, awakening parts of her body she had forgotten existed. "And," he continued, "I'd be lying if I said I wanted to do anything other than to make love to you tonight, Laney."

"Gee, you do tell it like it is," she said breathily.

He went in for another kiss, this one more probing and delicious than before, perhaps a preview of what making love meant to him. Whatever the motivation, Laney turned to gelatin.

The situation was beyond hope. "Back to your hotel room it is, then."

Tie had a three-room suite at the Radisson, with pastel colors similar to those from the conference room. Laney stood in the middle of the sitting area, staring out the window since the ombre curtains had been left open. The city was still alive beneath them, the rows and columns of lights above reminders that much was also going on behind closed doors.

"So, NPR treats its hosts pretty well, huh?"

"Yes, it does. But if you're referring to the suite, I paid for it myself."

Laney turned her head. "Why?"

He shrugged. "Because I could. And I felt like it. I can be unpredictable."

She walked toward the kitchenette area. "I can't say I've been in many suites. Despite all my conference traveling, my colleagues and I usually don't end up in these unless we share." She chuckled. "I guess I wouldn't mind my WYQT donation going to help its staff travel in comfort. Although I guess you're not a WYQT report—"

Tie spun her around and covered her mouth with his, guiding them into a gentle but increasingly intense kiss.

"I don't want to talk about suites, or conferences, or much else, Laney," he said, his heart pounding against her. "Why don't we give our vocab a break and let our bodies take over communication from here?"

Clearly, it was more a declaration than a suggestion, as he took her by the hand and led her to the bedroom. Laney silently thanked Nette for talking her into wearing sexy lingerie. She pulled her hair to the front while he gently unzipped her and kissed her bare shoulder.

"It's taking all my self-control not to rip things off of you," he whispered.

"Thank you," she whispered back, turning to him as her Chanel dress slipped to the floor.

She had purchased it at a consignment shop, but it still wasn't cheap. Stepping out of her dress, she pulled his head down to hers. Their tongues were in a heated dance, and as much as Laney enjoyed it, she was being driven out of her mind in her need for more. His hardness against her seemed to underscore the fact that he belonged deep inside of her. The rotation of the earth depended on it. As soon as possible. The creamy wetness in her red-and-black lace panties was further evidence of that.

And Tie was clearly a step or two ahead of her, landing

her on the bed before she knew it.

She lay stretched out on the crisp, white sheet, feeling remarkably comfortable under this man's gaze. His eyes shone, almost catlike, in the dim lights. His hunger was apparent. She felt like an alluring goddess, a foreign feeling she basked in.

"You're incredibly sexy. Irresistible." His stare did not leave her as he undressed, and she relished having an uninterrupted view as he unveiled his hard, sand-colored body, including a somewhat intimidating-looking erection.

Oh. For the second time, she silently thanked Nette. "Um, I have condoms in my purse, in the sitting area."

He was back to the foot of the bed in less than a minute, fully sheathed. He crawled onto the bottom of the bed and started at her feet, kissing every one of her toes. Laney felt the electric tingles deep in her core. He was going to drive her to the brink without even penetrating her. She tried to let her thoughts go, tried to stay in the moment, to fully enjoy this new experience with her fantasy man. She felt sexy. How wonderful to feel sexy in a natural, non-seedy way. Without endless pairs of hungry eyes roaming over her bare flesh.

He slowly kissed the sides of her calves and then moved toward her sensitive inner thighs, going back and forth between them. It had been a long time since she experienced this level of sensuality. Too long. She writhed.

"Oh, Tie," she whispered.

As he neared the apex of her thighs, his tongue poked through his lips when he kissed her and she squirmed, moaning as her heart rate quickened. He slowly pulled off her panties, yet he didn't explore her most sensitive areas, which were ready with a wet and warm welcome. He kissed his way up her pelvis and around her belly button, took it gently between his teeth and swirled his tongue around it. He continued creating a trail of soft kisses toward her chest.

She let out a long sigh.

He gently unhooked her bra and tossed it to the side. He explored each of her breasts with his soft, full lips, using his tongue on each nipple, gently kissing, sucking, nibbling, and swirling. Laney swore to herself that he must have been escorting her to heaven as she writhed and sighed. Warmth increased in her core and built toward a climax, but he continued his mission and she went back to enjoying each new sensation as he kissed the sides of her neck, her jaw, and then paused above her face, looking deeply into her eyes.

His were darker than ever and dynamic, even in the dimness. She reveled in the weight of his body against hers as she waited for his next move. She wrapped her legs around him, bringing him closer. His hot stiffness was against her belly, and her breaths quickened. His tongue slid into her mouth, softly at first but then with more command as he expertly explored her mouth, his tender lips caressing hers. Their tongues wrestled; she was desperate to taste the inside of his mouth, and the warmth in her core spread down her legs.

She needed him deep inside of her, delving into her depths as his tongue was doing to her mouth. She widened her legs and gently tried to guide his manhood toward her center, but her gesture sent him crawling downward instead. She gasped as his tongue penetrated her and his thumb gently circled her wet and hardened nub. She cried out as he withdrew his tongue, replaced it with two fingers, and let his restless tongue take over stroking and massaging her increasingly sensitive bud, alternating soft and moderate pressure.

"Yes, Tie! Oh, my god. Ooohhhhh!" She soared toward a climax, and just when it seemed inevitable he stopped and crawled back onto her, again looking deeply into her eyes.

"Ready for me?"

"God, yes, Tie! Please!"

"I'm so ready for you." He gently pushed into her, and Laney cried out as she tried to accommodate his thickness.

She stretched quickly with each of his exploring thrusts. He pushed farther into her, grunting softly. He was near fully in; Laney grabbed his ass and pulled him hard into her, moaning with the satisfying feeling of fullness.

"Oh, shit." He gasped.

He rocked in and out; Laney welcomed the strong tension expanding through her pelvis and inner thighs, relished the delicious friction. Her nails dug into his back, and she kissed and bit his neck as he groaned in her ear.

He used his well-defined arms to flip them over so that she was sitting breathlessly on top of him.

"Don't worry." He panted. "I won't make you do all the work." He began to thrust upward, powerfully, and his tight abs clenched.

She sat back a little, enjoying his taking charge. He rubbed against parts of her she didn't know existed.

She began to moan loudly. "Tie, Tie, yes." Every time she thought she'd hit her peak, the intensity would build again, like riding the waves of an ocean of ecstasy. He reached up and stroked between her legs at the precise, most combustible place.

"Omigod, Tie!" A sea of pleasure crashed into her as she contracted and shuddered, and she wished the sensation would never leave her. "Yes, please!" she begged.

When she began to descend from the summit of nirvana, she opened her eyes and her vision blurred. But she was very much aware of her dream man, who was still making love to her.

"Your body's speaking to me." He groaned loudly, grabbed her by the hips, and furiously guided her up and down until he, too, let out a cry and slowed his movements. She collapsed on him, her head on his chest as they tried to catch their breaths. He lifted her head gently and stared into her eyes. She inched up toward him and they shared a luxurious kiss.

"That was spectacular!" Tie exclaimed.

Laney could not speak. Her mind was still whirling, her body still melting into his. What was his secret? Was she just that infatuated with him? Or had he put a spell on her?

"ARE YOU FUCKING kidding me?" Tie was on his back a while later, chest heaving, and slid his fingers into his hair for a moment before yanking them back out in a gesture of disbelief. "Wow. Fucking wow. That was even better than the last time. I wouldn't have thought that possible."

Her ears grew hot, even in her sexually induced reverie. It was a wonder there was enough blood left to create that reaction.

"Goddamn, damn, damn. Girl! How did you do that to me? How are you so sexy? You're astonishing. It was heaven." His hand stroked the side of her face.

Laney chuckled. "It's kind of fun to hear expletives coming out of your usually refined mouth." It was true. But the unexpected words from her date—date! He was her idol—were still somehow poetic, rich, and definitely titillating. Even his flurry of words as he orgasmed belonged on an R&B album. And as for herself, she had no idea that she was such a loud moaner during sex. Being with Tie just one night had taught her new things about herself.

"If I fantasized about us—and I definitely have—it couldn't have been any better, Laney."

She shyly looked at his profile, waiting for him to come out from his own sexual intoxication enough to realize that this was real. She was very real and lying right next to him. She needed him to come down because she needed the affirmation herself. That the whole experience, from the sushi dinner to the feel of soft sheets tangled around her, was not fantasy. Not a daydream, as usual, but tangibly real. Real enough she could literally feel his voice, deep and silky, as he whispered in her ear. She found her fingers gently stroking his chin, and she relished in the barely noticeable but delicious feel of new stubble starting to form.

Enticing green eyes settled on her, making her heart speed up, and she reflexively jerked her hand away. He smiled, illuminating his face, and gently brought her hand back, allowing her to caress his jaw. His pupils were still large, making his eyes a bit smoky, and yet his excited irises sparkled as much as ever.

Tracing her lips with his thumb, he crooned, "You are phenomenal."

She was no phenom. But this, this night… this was definitely a phenomenon. One that she was trying to drink in as faithfully as possible, so she could relive it for years to come. Laney had no clue whether she would ever again see this man. But odds seemed against it.

"I never do that. This," she whispered, pulling the sheet up to her and all around her. "Um, I mean, I never do this sex-on-a-first-date thing."

He smiled and looked at her hands clutching the soft hotel sheet.

He wrapped his fingers around hers and tugged down slightly. "May I?"

She tentatively loosened her fingers and told herself to calm down and act cool.

He gently peeled the sheet away again and his beautiful dark lashes seemed to brush his cheeks as he looked her over. She felt chills as his gaze came to rest on hers. This was real. She saw the gold flecks in his adoring eyes and the smallest freckle to the left of his left iris, details she wasn't imaginative enough to dream up. But how on earth could this be?

She was pulled back to her full senses when his soft warm

lips met hers and her core stirred again, despite seeming to have been rendered to pudding with exhausting pleasure just moments before. His eyes were still open, which further reeled her in. *He's a mind reader.* He was trying to pull her fully into his world, like in the '80s A-ha "Take on Me" video where the pencil-sketched guy pulled the woman into his living, penciled world, and together they ran…

She sank into Tie, who closed his eyes and let his hand glide down her back, brush past her butt, and pull up her leg so he could start exploring her again. They entwined and melted together, setting the night to a steady, private rhythm that she would memorize by heart.

LANEY OPENED HER eyes, momentarily disoriented. Then it all came back to her, right up to Tie's insistence that she stay the night and his waking her up at some hour in the morning for their fourth round of lovemaking and spooning in the afterglow. Dear god, it had all really happened. The slight hangover ache in her head further attested to that.

And it would now really be ending. Surprisingly, her eyes stung with tears and she blinked rapidly, staving them off. They had no place in a one-night stand, even if it involved someone with whom she'd had a one-way "relationship," on some level, for two years.

On the other hand, maybe this was a blessing. What had taking any of her previous relationships beyond one date done for her? Spending time with Tie for one magical night would keep her memories unspoiled by the disappointment or heartache that inevitably seemed to come with time. If she left now, she would maintain an unblemished relationship with Tie, even if it was through radio airwaves and fantasy.

She turned, allowing herself one last close-up of his perfect face, and was surprised to see his eyes open and fastened on her. He had a small smile on his face.

"You're awake! Why didn't you wake me?"

"Why should I? I kept you up last night; the least I can do is allow you to sleep in a little. "Besides," he said, glancing at the bedside clock. "My flight isn't until eleven thirty." He propped himself up on his elbow and moved ringlets out of her face with his other hand. "Would you like to have breakfast? I could order room service so you wouldn't have to rush."

"Oh, Tie." Laney sat up, covering herself with the sheets. "It's a workday, you know? I have to get my head back in the game. And I've been greedy enough with your time." What she really wanted was to get the good-bye over with sooner rather than later.

"Okay, beautiful, I respect that. I just wanted to enjoy every possible minute with you while I'm here. But I know it's complicated." He looked disappointed. Then the disappointment was replaced by a glint in his sexy greens.

He tugged at the top of her sheet. "May I?"

She sighed. Sober, she was even shyer about displaying her naked self. "This again? Okay, sure."

The sheet dropped, leaving her feeling like a nude model, particularly as he eyed every visible inch of her, then his fingers trailed his gaze. When his fingers dipped again for a little more intense, intimate exploration, Laney immediately went full throttle again. Jesus, this was hopeless! Could she not follow through on her rational decisions with him around?

Yet when he sat up and lifted her atop him, she willingly, hungrily saddled him and slowly reintroduced her soft, increasingly wet core to his thick, hot, rock-hardness. Round five was a fulfilling breakfast that took her mind off of headaches and heartaches.

Chapter Four

HE CLOSED HIS eyes. He had been with a fair share of women, but never had he experienced sex like he'd had with Laney. Their bodies seemed made for each other. Though he previously would have rolled his eyes at such a statement, it was the only thing that made sense to him at present. It went beyond physical ecstasy, although that was certainly in the mix. She took him on a ride to another dimension. He only hoped she had a similar experience.

Her soft curves, smooth brown skin, luscious lips, and gorgeous eyes. Her delicate touch, taste, and amazing smell, the sweet moans and gasps coming from her mouth—he tried to lock all of these memories in his mind. Then he quickly opened his eyes. He couldn't allow himself to get too excited. He was wearing stylish, snug pants, and the last thing he needed was for his producer to notice an obvious bulge in them. Awkward.

Outside the airplane window, wispy white whirls were painted on cerulean blue, and the sun rays illuminating the picture reminded him of her. She had made an indelible impression, and that was before sex. During dinner, when he could have confessed that he was a college dropout, he dodged the subject. Although he'd had a fleeting sense that she might not care. She was already impressed. And she was interested in so many other aspects of his story.

But she was a psychologist. She was probably interested in anyone's story. He'd keep the dropout fact under wraps if he saw her again.

He had to see her again.

And he could. WYQT, Columbus, was very soon to become the home station for *Biz-E Life*. Though he'd thus far not been especially looking forward to the move, he now felt a little more excited about the prospect. There wasn't much else to balance the equation. He would be leaving behind his dear sister, friends, and the town he had grown to love. But his attraction to Laney was a plus in favor of the move.

He just had to see her again.

So why hadn't he told her about the upcoming move? *I do want to see her again, don't I?*

He looked over at his lead producer, who was immersed in a book. Blue was always mellow—that was what made her a great producer to work with. He wanted to ask her how she honestly felt about the show's move, but she looked so intent on her reading, he left her alone. He needed to shake off his thoughts about Laney, though, or he'd go nuts.

TIE LOOKED OVER the rough sketch of his fundraising plan for his idea of a financial literacy camp for youth. Yes, he was going to need a lot of help, and he had not yet established a social network in Columbus. His cousin Joe had given him the name of a couple of promising bigwigs so he had a start. He could also count on people at the radio stations, since they were very familiar with fundraising. And his ace in his back pocket was the number of connections he'd made with guests on his program. Somehow, this would all come together. Tie was optimistic. He had a solid reputation in the Chicago area, indeed nationally. It would not be difficult to maintain a well-respected image in Columbus.

It would take a lot of work. But if he wanted to pilot the program next summer, he had to get moving. It was nearly autumn. Fortunately, his new job wasn't really a new job at all. So, knowing those ropes opened up time and mental space for securing funds. He planned to delegate a good deal. He had already enlisted the services of a grant writer to target and propose the plan to various funders. He also planned to hire an event planner for his big fund-raising event, a gala. This was what he was engaged in now, at the desk in his WLAK office. Researching various event planners online and calling those who looked promising. No one was in the lead when Blue came by and stuck her head in his office. He suddenly switched windows on his screen, feeling a bit guilty for taking care of other business at work.

Blue didn't seem to notice or care. "Hi there. Everything set for the show?"

"Okay on my end. Yours?"

"Some sticky fact-checking issues, but I think we've smoothed out the kinks." She leaned against the doorframe. "You know we're gonna miss you around here, right? The station just won't be the same."

"Oh, you won't be able to get away from my voice at six thirty, so I believe you're actually stuck with me." Tie smiled. He was touched that the staff would be throwing him a small going-away party tomorrow.

"And as your friend, I wish you nothing but happiness." She paused. "It's perhaps not my place to say, but I'm glad that you broke up with Amy. She was weighing you down. You seem lighter now. You need someone who will help you to maintain that liveliness and discover self-potentials you aren't aware of."

Tie turned his chair to fully face her. "So now you're my little sister? Or is it big sister?" Tie was not good at gauging people's ages.

Blue shared a Mona Lisa smile. "Just a friend who hopes to stay your friend. Reach out to me, to us, if you need anything, Tie. We know you're a deserving, stand-up guy."

A stand-up guy. There were worse ways to be remembered.

Chapter Five

L ANEY SAT BEHIND her desk, reading each email more than once. She could not bring her mind to focus.

Their parting kiss had been sweet but sensual, something that should have tided her over for at least a day, but she was already missing the taste of his mouth. During the kiss, she'd felt an uplift in her soul again, a transportation to somewhere unknown but exquisite. Was Xanadu really a thing? She tried to brush it off as her runaway imagination, part of the princess narrative.

She sighed and looked up as she heard a knock at her door. As usual, her glance served as an invitation for the student to come in. It was Alex, a very sweet sophomore in her psychopathology class this semester, and whom she remembered from introductory psych.

"Oh, hi, Alex. What can I do for you?"

He blushed. "Just wanted to see if I could get into your child development class."

Thank goodness she wasn't yet teaching. She wouldn't have been able to keep a lecture afloat today if her life depended on it. Well, maybe so. But, thankfully, she didn't need to wrestle with the challenge. Next week, however, all that would change.

"You sure you can deal with two of my classes?" Laney joked as she signed off on the appropriate paperwork.

Another knock on her door made her glance up again.

"Mind a slight interruption?" It was Tracey, a colleague in neuroscience.

Alex, flustered, hurriedly stood and threw his backpack over his shoulder. "Thanks for signing me in, Dr. Travers."

"You're welcome, Alex." Alex brushed past Tracey.

"That boy is on this floor, in your office again? You know he's one of our majors, not yours, right? I swear every time I dropped by last semester he was either hanging around outside your office or sitting or standing inside." Tracey neared Laney's desk and whispered. "Girl, he's crushing on you, hard. Better watch out for that."

"Oh, Alex is harmless." Laney waved the consideration away with her hand.

"Well," Tracey invited herself to sit down. "I could just have easily emailed, but Fitbit reminded me that I needed to get my ass up and walk anyway. So here I am."

Laney laughed. "So I guess I can look forward to seeing you on a more frequent basis." She wouldn't mind. Tracey was one of the other few Black women faculty members at the college, and they had developed an easy friendship.

"Wait a minute. Something about you looks different." Tracey eyed Laney's hair and blazer before finally looking back at her face. "Hmmm. You don't really wear much makeup, so it's not that... but it *is* your face." She gasped. "Girl, you got laid!" she "whispered" loudly.

"Shhhhhhhh!!" Laney answered in an even louder whisper.

Tracey's hand clamped over her own mouth. "Sorry. I was just shocked. But it's true, right?"

Laney rolled her eyes and barely gave a nod, with a fleeting wonder at how on earth her friend had determined this from looking at her face. Was she radiating like a neon sign?

Tracey jumped up excitedly and closed the door to Laney's office.

"These are my office hours," Laney protested.

"They can wait a minute. Nobody uses office hours anyway. It's email, unless they're crushing on you. Now," she sat down again. "Tell, tell, tell!"

"I'd really rather not. It was just a… thing… but kind of a complicated thing I don't want to get in to explaining right now." She twisted her hands beneath her desk. "I'm really just trying to forget about it."

Tracey looked disappointed. "That bad? Hmm. So it's just business as usual, then? Well, maybe over coffee in a few days?"

Laney shrugged. "We'll see where my head's at."

"Well, girl, I'm sorry if things went downhill, but something must have gone right, because you wear the afterglow well!"

Laney's face warmed and she had a desperate need to change the subject. "What did you come by to discuss?"

"Oh. Well, small potatoes compared to one of us actually getting some action. But, just a reminder about our idea of providing an info/social capital program for first-year students from disadvantaged backgrounds. Mostly minority students but also some first-gen or lower-income White students. You remember our discussing this, right?" She stood and reopened Laney's door before returning to her seat. The college's open-door policy was well ingrained.

"Uh... yes, but I haven't given it any more thought, honestly. I've had a lot on my plate."

"No doubt. But that's why I wanted to come by and get the bug back in your ear early on."

Laney moved uncomfortably in her seat. "I really want to get it started, but I don't know that I'll have the time for all the planning, let alone running it. I mean, I'd have to learn some of the information myself!" Laney tried not to think about the fact that they were inspired to create such a program because they could have used one when they had started college. She didn't want to feel like she was turning her back on the important subject. Coming from a disadvantaged background, knowing how to navigate some aspects of college like student loans would have helped tremendously.

Tracey looked somewhat disappointed again. "It's just that you seemed so enthusiastic about the idea."

"Still am. It's very important. But I think proposing it is the extent to which we need to go. Then... we can move on to something else less time-consuming. Another bit of service to add to the vita," she said.

She immediately regretted it. Though teaching and scholarship were the most important skills in which to shine, everyone knew that some degree of service to the college was expected in order to obtain tenure. But for her to lump this potentially important program in with "checkmarks toward tenure" rather than valuable in its own right was shameful.

"Well, true. I do have other ideas I'm invested in, and it is indeed a bonus they'll add lines to the CV." Tracey's hazel eyes sparkled again. "Let's talk about them sometime when you're not pressed for time?"

"You've got it."

Chapter Six

HE WOULD MISS his spacious loft near downtown Chicago, but a friend had already helped him to find an impressive condo in the Columbus suburbs for an unbelievable price. Ohio had its perks. He had hired the same excellent moving company he'd used previously, so as far as he was concerned, he was practically already settled in Columbus. The stations and NPR staff were dealing with all the pragmatics of moving the show, and he was glad he would be able to retain most of his staff, including Blue, though they'd be in a different city.

There was still an area he felt less certain about, however. He had been tossing around the idea of starting the financial literacy camp for years. The debt that his college buddies had racked up—especially his friends from low-income or racial/ethnic minority backgrounds—was staggering. And the fact that credit card companies had preyed upon college students at that time only worsened their situations. They were still in massive debt today. He had learned how lucky he was to have parents who taught him the value of a dollar, and who explained things like interest to him early. The idea of a camp had grown particularly clearer in the last year or so.

"You are missing a golden opportunity, man," Craig said after sipping his beer. They were sitting outside on a lovely late summer day, watching young, laughing bright-eyed students and harried businesspeople walking by them as they sat in front of a popular bar. They were on the north side of Chicago, Lincoln Avenue in Lincoln Park.

"And you're missing the point. I'm not interested in helping people who already have money or those who need some money management tips. There are folks already out there doing that, making a good name for themselves as well as a few bucks. That's great. And, eventually, I might start my own similar business, but it will have a different slant. Right now, though, I'm focused on kids. Getting high school students the information they need to make better financial choices—starting now."

Craig sighed. "You never conformed to the business-man's ways, did you? Always concerned with information, giving it away. Nonprofit style."

"Yeah. Why not? Information is critical capital. So I'm gonna submit some grants, find some funding so that this might be a remote possibility, and I'll go from there."

"I don't know of a single sixteen-year-old who would be interested in attending a day camp—especially one focused on finance. You're really stuck in your bubble, aren't you?"

Tie's stomach tightened and his face grew hot, but he kept his tone even. "My job takes me outside the bubble a lot, thank you. And like I said, student debt is a real thing."

"You always were a bleeding heart! Here…" He raised his glass. "To saints everywhere. May they make the world a better place."

Tie perfunctorily raised his glass, realizing that his friend was well on his way to drunk. No sense talking about it to him. He needed to be talking to people who could actually help him.

He'd get busy once he got to Columbus.

Later that day, Tie absentmindedly picked up a bourbon glass. Laney had his number—would she call him? Somehow, they parted without her having shared her own information. But he thought they had a real connection. Not only in sync in minds and in bed, but another attraction that transcended explanation. It was a sensation he felt whenever they lightly touched. Like they lit each other up. Or, at least, she lit him up. Perhaps she didn't experience the same thing.

It was my fault. He was carefully packing his bar. Glasses were wrapped in newspaper and his expensive liquor nestled in Styrofoam. Why hadn't he told her that he would be moving to Columbus? No wonder she was no longer interested. She thought she'd never see him again. Maybe he wasn't ready to hear whether or not she wanted to see him a second time. He perceived the evening as very special, and he didn't want to spoil the memory.

But, god, he wanted to see her again.

He tried to track her down but to no avail. Finally he found an email address and wrote a note—which he spent an hour on trying to figure out how to word. He wanted to convey his desire but not come across as too stalker-ish. He could just state that he'd be moving to Columbus, but that sounded too impersonal. Finally he just went with…

Dear Laney,

I hope you don't mind. I found your email address on your Sheffield web page. I wanted to reconnect with you after our fantastic evening together. I'm hoping that we can see each other again now that I am moving to Columbus! I'll announce it on the show at the end of the week, but I wanted you to be the first listener to know. If you don't mind passing along your phone number, perhaps I can give you a call? I hope to speak with you soon.

Best,
Tie

After a pause he added "Stevens." Who knew? And with a deep breath, he pressed send. His heart was thumping and his mouth was dry. He would never have thought he could become so anxious over a woman. But this wasn't just any woman.

DURING THE NEXT week, Laney hesitated before calling on her students, fearing she would call them by Tie's name. Three days after he left, she had to stop listening to *Biz-E Life*. Clearly his voice wasn't enough, and yet it was too much at present. With the thirty minutes freed, she was able to throw herself more into her work. This was good, because it seemed to take her twice as long to do anything, given the added distraction. She shelved his autographed book, tucked his business card somewhere she knew she'd forget, and tried to erase him with the occasional glass of wine, but it didn't seem to "take." When would all this obsessing go away?

It had been no ordinary one-night stand, whatever that even meant. Even if she'd had a one-night stand with Idris Elba, she wouldn't be as preoccupied with thoughts of him. She'd probably be riding the elation for a little while, and then eventually just have vague, fond memories.

And the thing was, she should have been glad that it was a one-night stand. This way she would not have to deal with the drama of a relationship as she was busy preparing for tenure. Especially an interracial relationship, which would probably bring complications of its own. But she found herself yearning for another night with Tie.

Her best friend had noticed the changes in Laney, and did what she could to try to comfort her, in her own unique way. Laney almost felt bad for bumping Nette into the role of the nurturer, since it was clearly a difficult role for her. Nette's brusqueness had almost ended their friendship when Laney lost her mother a few years prior. So she tried to be as normal as possible around Nette, but it apparently wasn't working.

Nette's ways had softened some with aging, however. Her latest attempt was a gift certificate for a mani-pedi. Laney smiled, knowing it must have been a pleasure for Nette to buy her less-than-girly friend something frilly.

As she and Nette sat with their hands under the dryers, Laney couldn't help but wish there was a certain man around to admire the lilac on her nails and the baby blue on her toes.

Nette had dictated the colors, knowing Laney would have otherwise gone for matching neutrals. But, as it was, the cheerful colors stood in contrast to her mood. She hoped her smile and laughter was enough to fool Nette, if not herself.

Chapter Seven

A SMALL PART of Tie expected to hear from Laney, since he announced the show's move to Columbus a couple of times now. He was half hoping she would call, while the other half of him was reserved, not allowing his expectations to get ahead of him.

But he still had the drive to see her again. He managed to track down her phone number after bouncing from one person to the next. He was just nervous about attempting the call.

He dialed the number.

"Hello?" The curiosity in her voice suggested that she was unfamiliar with the Chicago area code. In any case, she would not know his number, unless she had programmed it into her phone.

He took a breath. "Laney."

"Y-yes. Tie." The endearing quiver had returned to her voice.

"It's been a while. Let me get right to it. How are you feeling about my coming to Columbus?" He couldn't keep the excitement out of his voice.

"What? I don't understand. Are you coming for another meeting? I don't recall you mentioning anything a few weeks ago." He couldn't identify what it was about her voice that conveyed displeasure, but it threw him off course.

"Laney? Haven't you been listening to the radio? Not that I think my show is essential to your life, but I got the impression that you were a loyal listener. I've been announcing the show's move to our sister station in Columbus for a few days now!"

"Uh, I haven't had time to listen to the radio." She sounded uncertain.

"Oh." This seemed odd to him, but he chalked it up to her likely busyness with the semester having started. "Yeah, anyway, it's true. I'm moving to Columbus! Like, this weekend." He paused, wondering whether she was ready to hear what was on his mind. "You don't know how much I've thought about you."

"I have to go. Um, I'm glad this worked out for you. You really seem happy to be moving here." Her voice sped up, and she seemed to be rushing him off the phone.

He felt like someone had punched him in the stomach. "Laney? Are you—"

"I really do need to run. Maybe we'll catch up later. Bye." She hung up.

Tie held the phone to his ear for a full minute afterward. *What the hell?* She really had relegated him to a one-night stand, and thus was not pleased to hear from him. Nothing else made sense.

But, he had to make sure.

A FEW DAYS later, Laney was showing a video clip in which kids were guessing how much colored water was in different sized containers, and comparing them. Her students had been enraptured, as they usually were by this clip, but now their attention seemed to be drawn toward the door. Laney glanced in that direction and was shocked to see Tie standing outside, off to the side. She swiftly turned back to the video, regained her composure, and managed to stay focused for the next ten minutes left of class.

Tie waited patiently as students filed out, some of them looking at him curiously, still others, especially the young women, simply stared before nudging each other and giggling. Laney noted all of this out of the corner of her eye while she spoke with a couple of students who had questions for her after class.

When the last student left, she tentatively glanced in Tie's direction. It would be silly to pretend she hadn't seen him. Yet he seemed to be waiting for a direct invitation.

She took a deep, uneven breath. "Come on in, Tie."

He smiled and her legs started to turn to jelly. She propped herself up on the podium just to be sure she didn't make a fool of herself. Dammit. His smile was still a stunner. As were his eyes. Hell, he was a gorgeous package. She'd thought she'd memorized every detail of his face, but Tie in the flesh eclipsed Tie in her imagination. Her spine fell away.

"Professor Travers."

She tried to avoid his eyes.

"Laney. I'm sorry to just show up at your workplace. I tried phoning you again, but you weren't returning my calls."

Had he missed the glaring hint?

"And maybe it's because you didn't want to talk to me, after all." He came closer, and Laney smelled his familiar scent, which weakened her further. "But, is there another class in here now?"

Laney shook her head.

"Listen," he whispered, coming yet closer. "I believe that we had—have—a connection too strong to be tossed away for lack of communication."

Laney met his eyes. His hubris was too much. Had she fallen for a pompous ass? No, she could not allow herself to be the girl who let a man skate responsibility simply because he was charming. Oh, hell no. "Yet, you're the one who failed to communicate with me, leaving me with just your memory. How do you expect me to respond when you're suddenly just like, 'I'm back!'"

Tie gently put his hands on her shoulders. The sensation of his hands on her whirled through her like a delicious, warm breeze, and the pleasant lightness returned. She tried to ignore it. *Ground yourself, Laney.*

"Laney, honey, I can explain all that if you just give me a chance. Doesn't that seem sensible?"

Dammit. He was appealing to rationality when she was just coming out of professor mode. And hearing "honey" on his tongue made her feel… like royalty.

But what if a student or colleague saw them in what could be construed as an intimate encounter? She didn't need rumors flying around. She shrugged off his hands and, in order to soften that blow, conceded, "I guess it makes sense. I have time for a brief chat somewhere. I'm actually running late for a meeting now, but maybe we can meet at someplace. Where did you move to?"

Tie grinned. Damn that smile. "Bexley. But the movers are arriving the day after tomorrow, so they say. So I'm back at the Radisson."

"Okay, eight o'clock at the hotel bar sound okay?"

"Yes, Professor." Tie looked ready to lean toward her, but he didn't.

She breathed a barely audible sigh of relief. Thank goodness he hadn't gone there. That surely would have been an awkward moment.

Laney went downtown directly after finishing some work at her office and arrived a little early. No harm in getting a head start. She should get her thoughts together before Tie arrived.

"Dirty martini, please," she passed along to the attractive male hotel bartender.

A tall, thin man in a dark gray shirt and tie, wrinkle-free trousers and jacket slung over his back sidled up beside Laney. He smiled briefly at her, though long enough to peruse her top half. Laney felt self-conscious in her white silk blouse, although it was matched with a modest pair of charcoal slacks. From Tall Man's perspective, though, no doubt her cleavage was showcased.

When he had the bartender's attention, he said, "I'll have a Glenfiddich, neat. And what has the young lady ordered?"

"Dirty martini."

"On one bill, please."

Tall Man turned to Laney, looking rather smug. The lights shone in his black hair, which was slicked back and held perfectly in place. There was something untrustworthy about his smile, and his whole vibe was not suiting her. "You're very pretty. What are you doing here alone?"

Laney was irritated, but she didn't refuse the free martini. Sipping it, she said, "I'm meeting my… a… someone."

Tall Man looked amused. "Your someone. Hmmm. Well, I'm just waiting for a business associate. Taking him to La Chatelaine and then showing him the best of what Columbus nightlife has to offer. The latter part sounds deceptively fun, but it's a lot of work to find good spots, especially since I'm from New York. We probably won't get very far."

Laney affected a knowing smile in return, continuing to sip.

"So what do you do?" He continued looking her over, not bothering to hide his lust. "I'm Cal, by the way."

She accepted his hand, which was remarkably soft. "Laney. I'm a professor. Down at Sheffield, just outside of the city."

"Good school. Good business preparation. We hire students right out of Sheffield." He stared at her.

He must have been waiting for her to ask him where he worked, etc. But she didn't care.

Instead, Laney mustered a wooden smile. Small talk wasn't her favorite thing, anyway. She started to look around for Tie and found him walking toward them, looking somewhat disgruntled.

"Well, Cal. Good to meet you. This is my… someone. Thanks for the drink."

Cal glanced in Tie's direction, held his scotch up in salute and turned to look around—probably to see whether there were any other single women he could approach in the sparsely populated bar.

"You seemed to get chummy. Am I that late?"

"No. It doesn't take long for anyone to start talking about himself over drinks." She indicated to the bartender that she was ready for her second martini. She could use the liquid courage for whatever this conversation would entail. "Tie? What do you want to drink?"

When she was settled with her second drink and he had his frosty glass of beer, he turned and looked her fully in the eyes. She didn't resist his gaze. She would be firm.

"Hi, Laney. You look stunning, as always."

"Hi." Curses! For some reason she felt shy. It was his piercing green eyes, perhaps. He just wouldn't stop being drop-dead gorgeous any time soon, so she had to just try regrowing her spine. "Thank you. You're looking well yourself."

"First, I want to say that I'm so glad you agreed to meet with me because I've missed you very much. Seriously, I would have shown up in one of your classes one day if I couldn't get to you. Front row."

She laughed despite herself. Coming from any other man, such a statement would have spooked her. But hearing this from Tie was satisfying.

"So, the main thing I want to say is that I'm sorry." He had a long drink of his beer. "I guess I'm not good at the start of relationships—at least, in my mind we have a relationship. I either come on too strong or come off like the Invisible Man. I don't wish to be either of those guys." He tentatively put his hand on her knee, and his scintillating touch sent shivers down her spine and precipitously lowered her defenses.

"I do know that I wanted to keep mum about moving here until the deal was definitely in place. I should have told you then. But something occurred to me. What if she doesn't care? Wasn't I being awfully self-assured? In which case, wouldn't it make sense to give it another week or so after I started announcing it on the air? At which point, if you did give a damn, well, wouldn't you call me? After all, you had my personal card. I had nothing of yours."

Wait. What was going on here? Suddenly she felt on the defensive, although she couldn't say that she was experiencing Tie's words as an attack, exactly. "You knew where I work."

"Hold on, Laney." Tie rubbed her knee. "When I didn't hear from you I came to the conclusion that you weren't calling because you were angry with me for some reason or you had no desire to maintain any kind of relationship." He reached for his beer and took a sip, with a look on his face that married frustration and hopelessness. "I just wasn't ready to entertain that thought. Still, I was determined enough that I had to reach you. It took me a while to track you down and call you. You're not easy. There are two

Elaines at your school, so the automatic phone system didn't handle that too well. I did get the other Elaine, who for some reason referred me to your friend Nenette instead of your office number, and that's how I got your cell phone number." He paused to take a few sips. "I did email you, though. At least at the address I found on your website." He cocked his head.

She would have remembered seeing his name in her in-box. That would have made her day. "Could have landed in one of my clutter management folders." She sighed, regretting falling behind in scanning her clutter folders.

"Well, anyway. I don't know if I'm allowed to tell you, but Nenette was all too thrilled to give up your number."

Perhaps this was Nette's exciting news from last week that she hadn't yet had the chance to share.

Laney, who had been listening rather than talking, was nearly completed with her second drink. "A third for the lady?" The bartender smiled. She shook her head and returned his smile.

"Yes, well, I'll have to have a talk with Nette about dos and don'ts with my number."

"So you are angry? Disappointed?" He looked away. "Not interested?"

She slowly munched on an olive. "I might have been angry earlier, but listening to you now, I guess I'm just disappointed. Maybe disappointed in the both of us." She unexpectedly chuckled, hand up to mouth. "Not so grown-up now, are we?"

"I beg to differ." He turned to her, then tentatively bent

and kissed her on the cheek.

"Well, we've done some very grown-up things, but our emotional connection has perhaps not yet quite caught up with our physical connection." Her breath was shallow, affected by the kiss.

He kissed her other cheek. "So, we forgive ourselves; remain patient enough to make room for error… if it's worth it to you."

Worth it to her? He was her fantasy lover. "Tie?" Her eyes widened.

"Mm-hmm?"

"You're really back? For real?"

"For real."

She reached up and brought his head down to hers, reuniting them in a long-awaited kiss. Though she was still seated, her knees weakened as his tongue tenderly danced with hers, and his soft lips kept them connected. This felt completely natural. Their connecting in this way felt right.

"Wanna go talk some more upstairs?" he queried into her mouth.

"Yes," she whispered into his.

They pulled apart and he fished around in his wallet.

She allowed him to pull her to the elevator even as her nerves started to kick in. Would they still be in sync? Beyond the kiss they just shared? Would they pick up where they left off? Was she prepared for what might come afterward?

Tie led her into a suite similar to what he'd had previously. On the kitchen counter, there was a bottle of champagne on ice and a vase of beautiful deep pink roses.

He awaited her reaction, his hands in his pockets and looking sheepish.

She smiled and walked over to the counter. "It's very romantic."

"You mean, it's very presumptuous," he responded. "But, I figured if it didn't go so well downstairs, then you'd probably not make it up here to see my presumptive actions anyway." He smiled, a boyish, lady-killer smile. "I called room service to hook us up before I went on air."

He joined her by the counter and took out the champagne bottle. "May I?" He raised an eyebrow.

"But of course."

He popped the cork, wiped away the fizz, and poured Laney and himself full flutes. "To second chances." He raised his glass.

She raised hers. "To second chances, indeed." They clinked and she enjoyed the sweet asti tingle on her tongue. She then took a long drink, partly out of her nervousness, which was only just starting to dissipate, thanks to the two martinis.

"Whoa, easy there." He took her glass out of her hand and set his own down. "I want you lucid when I do this to you." He leaned forward and kissed her tenderly, around her mouth, on each of her lips, and then her whole mouth.

She savored the slow pace. Their tongues found a familiar rhythm and made Laney coo and press closer to him.

He pulled her chin away slightly. "You have no idea how long I've been agonizing over the next time I'd be able to do that," he said.

She smiled. "Oh, I have some idea, you can bet on that."

"Oh." He slipped one of the roses from the vase and caressed her on the nose with its soft petals.

The perfume was intensified by the wine on her palate. "Mmmm. Yummy," Laney said. "And lovely."

Tie studied her for a moment. "You appreciate them, but roses are not your favorite." How did he know that? "Well, I do adore them. But I guess white lilies have always been the belle of my ball when it comes to flowers. How did you—"

He replaced the rose. "Then white lilies you shall have, my dear. Now, where were we?"

Laney didn't have much more patience for scripts and role-playing. She grabbed Tie by the collar, took on his mouth with greedy kisses, and pushed him toward the love seat.

They killed one bottle of champagne between kisses, removing clothing and fondling each other. The sun had long set. Laney slipped her blouse on, did up a few of the buttons, and headed out the door with the empty ice bucket, preparing for more cold, flowing bubbly. Her shoes had long since been discarded, so she was feeling quite liberated. But no sooner had she began walking than she heard a familiar voice call out behind her. She turned around.

Tall Man Cal. And a tall, busty blonde woman hanging all over him. Judging from his gait, he was either drunk or high.

"Come join us, gorgeous! Right down the hall, you're going in the right direction. Corner suite at the end. We have coke. I think Cookie here even has some ecstasy. You can't keep slinging dirty martinis all night. Gotta keep the party going by staying awake!" He took two long strides and was standing across from her. The woman took a little longer to catch up in her five-inch heels, teetering on them in her own intoxicated state.

"No, thank you. I don't play around with that stuff."

"You're missing out, sweetheart." He took in her curves, his eyes glazed over with drugs and lust. "Oh, wait—you're with your... someone. Listen, baby, maybe this will sway you. I'm taller than him, so proportionally my hands and feet are bigger than his. I'll bet you a lifetime of oral sex that my cock is bigger than his."

Laney turned around. Her earlier perception of him as distasteful was on target. He was a horny jerk.

He reached out and grabbed her by the wrist, and she shook him off. He moved in front of her. "Seriously, girl, if you're going to be with a White guy, why would you get a man with a teenie weenie when you can get thick dick? You gotta know how to pick us out, sexy. You're all woman. You need a lot of man. God blessed me with a Black dude's cock."

Laney swung the empty ice bucket at him and made contact with his genitals.

"Shit! Bitch!" He doubled over.

The blonde woman cringed and looked at Laney with wide brown eyes.

"You want a line up?" Laney challenged, adrenaline coursing through her. "Drop your damn pants here and now. Come on, Magic Mike, show us what you're working with. I'm sure she'd like a sneak peek." Laney indicated the obvious sex worker still teetering in her heels.

Red crept up the back of Cal's neck.

The door opened; Tie glanced toward Cal and his neck muscles and jaw flexed. "Laney, are you okay?"

"Oh, honey, I'm more than okay," Laney said, a bit deliriously. "Cal here contends that he has the bigger penis—excuse me, cock—of the two of you, and so I told him to drop his damn pants. And, of course, all talk and no action." She glared at Cal.

Tie went into the hallway, glowering at Cal, who was still bent over, and gently took Laney back inside, bolting the door for extra measure. "Whew, milady!" He stared at her for a few moments. "You're no damsel in distress, are you? You took him right out!"

"I don't put up with it, Tie." She was pacing. "I can't just roll over and let filthy and racist remarks slide off my back. And it was an insult to you in the process."

"Whoa. He has filth dripping from him, I get that, but what racist remarks?"

"He said that if I was going to date White men, then I should essentially be picking ones with the biggest penises—like his, according to him. Retch." She stuck her finger down her throat.

Tie's face was red with fury and his hand was back on the knob.

"Oh no. You pulled me back in here, and that's a wrap."

"Listen, you." He approached her and cradled her face in his hands. "I don't want you seeing *anyone* else's penis as long as we're together. I hope we're clear on that, despite the fact that we haven't really had a discussion about it." He paused and dropped his hands. "Wow. That sounds really possessive."

Laney nodded slowly, privately elated. "It's okay. I agree. If we really want to give this a chance."

"And"—he took the ice bucket from her hand and put it on the counter—"I'm ruling that we've had enough for tonight."

"Okay. My stomach is starting to whirl a bit. I guess I'm starting to feel really giddy."

"Starting?"

"Okay, maybe for a little while. If we pushed it further, you could have your way with me, and we wouldn't want that."

Tie's shoulders slumped. "We wouldn't?"

Laney took a deep breath, trying to be as "sober" as possible. Tall Cal's words echoed in her head. "I want to start fresh with you. You know, we just sort of jumped into sex. I'd like some no-strings dating."

Tie put his fingers through the back of her thick, dark locks. "I think that's the point... our chemistry fated love-making. And the same will be for tonight. That's just how it is." He shrugged, looking pitiful before leaning down to release butterfly kisses on her neck, opening her blouse for more exposure.

She took a step back and put her hand on his chest. "Tie. No sex for now. Do you agree? Just to date for now and see where it takes us?"

His chest was heaving. He looked thoughtful. Slowly, he responded. "I guess that makes sense. We've had this misunderstanding lately and probably need the opportunity to see where our heads are. Although make-up sex would be hot right now, I will defer to your wisdom."

"So, I should probably head home, as much as I'd like to stay." She rebuttoned her blouse, avoiding his hypnotic eyes.

After slipping on her low heels and picking up her purse, she kissed him softly but intimately. She hoped she was conveying that she wanted to be with him, to give things a try. Given his smile after the kiss, she was successful.

Driving home, she thought about the evening. How remarkable things were now. So different from when she woke up with Tie those weeks ago. Then, she'd just hoped to retain in fine detail the memory of the glorious evening and morning. Now, she had much more. They had all but agreed to see no one else. Tie was hers—at least for now!

But her stomach began to tighten as she again recalled the situation with Tall Cal. Clearly, the bastard just wanted some Black pussy. She had experienced enough White men propositioning her after one of her dance sets, trying to "ride the rainbow," to add Laney to the list of other races and ethnicities they thought they had conquered. Tie was angry about the situation, but did he understand the racial nuances? For that matter—she couldn't stop the thought from occurring to her—was Tie possibly in this to win diversity points? Worse yet… was Tie mostly in this for the exotic erotic reasons she tried to avoid? She admitted to herself that these fears were a large part of the reason she had decided to call off sex for now.

In any case, if she continued to see him, she would be exposing herself to unpredictable perceptions by other Blacks. She could be considered a sellout to her race. To Black men. She wasn't crazy—she had been accused of such before. And that was just for being *friends* with a White guy. Heaven forbid she have lunch with a friend.

As the thoughts whirled around in her mind, she pulled up to her spot feeling a lot less elated now. Was this because she could think clearly out of his presence? She put her head on the steering wheel. So many questions. Not easy to determine the answers.

DEBBIE THE GOSSIP monger caught Laney in the copy room. "I'll wait," she said, leaning against the doorframe.

Oh no. She has something in mind. She hasn't even asked how long my copy job is.

"So, the students were gushing about some 'hottie'"—she actually did the air quotes—"who was talking to you the other day after class."

Laney kept focused on her work, pretending she hadn't heard anything of significance.

"Of course, I'm wondering whom and what they're talking about. So I tiptoed down the hall and looked into 211 and indeed there you were with some tall man who had you in his arms!"

It wasn't like that. She waited a couple of moments.

"That's my friend, actually. Came to speak to me after class was over and, no, I wasn't in his arms; he had his hands on my shoulders trying to emphasize something." Laney finished her job and finally met Debbie's eyes. "No big deal. Students forget we're not stationary ATMs, that we have friends and other lives. Seeing us as anything but professors is entertaining to them."

"So will we be seeing this… friend around in the future?"

Laney sped out of the room, pretending not to hear.

Debbie Thomas and her husband, Jeff, were hired as a package deal as assistant professors in the psychology department. They were hired a few years before Laney, so they were already tenured and had settled into their positions as if they were king and queen of the department. Debbie was full steam headed toward full professorship, publishing findings from her social psychology experiments at any chance she could, largely at the expense of teaching well.

Her husband was up to other things.

Laney walked past Jeff's office, hurrying to Amanda's, the administrative assistant, in order to retrieve some supplies from the closet. She held her head down, pretending to examine papers in her hand.

"La-aney," Jeff called.

Shoot. So close. Oh, well, she'd have to pass on the way back anyhow.

She took a couple of steps backward to appear in Jeff's doorway. "Yes?"

"Well, good morning! How are you?"

Laney put a hand on her hip. "I'm fine, Jeff. How are

you?"

Jeff didn't answer. Instead he took a sip from his coffee mug, as if it would camouflage his intentional gaze up and down her body, landing on her chest.

He put his mug down. "Yes, you are quite fine, aren't you?"

How was Laney supposed to respond to blatant leering from a senior colleague? His wife was in the copy room rather than in her office catty-corner to Jeff's, but her presence wouldn't have stopped his advances anyway. This was one of the more innocent situations, compared to his inappropriately brushing against Laney when ample space was available, or "accidentally" touching her behind. Her face would flame each time, and this time was no exception. She crossed her arms in front of her chest, using her papers as an extra shield, squared her jaw, and stared him down. "Did you want something, Jeff?"

"Just wanted to say good morning. You're always off in a rush."

"Well, there's a lot on my plate. Have a good—"

"Laney."

She raised her eyebrows.

"You look very nice today. That ensemble really flatters your... assets." He took the opportunity to look her up and down again, this time his gaze lingered on her hips.

He had a way of making her feel like she'd chosen an outfit from Frederick's of Hollywood rather than one of her usual conservative "uniforms."

"Thanks, Jeff. Well, have a good day." She scrambled

away before having to subject herself to any further harassment.

She felt like going home, taking a shower to get the "ick" off, and changing her clothes. Instead, her thoughts wandered.

She sashayed onto the stage, prepared for the bright lights that greeted her and showcased every millimeter of her glittering body. She wore clear acrylic five-inch heels and deep Pussy Pink on her toenails. The girls called her "butter feet" because her feet were so soft and smooth. Onstage she was Flower, the naughty fairy, with her diaphanous wings connected to her barely there bra. Her breasts jiggled and threatened to pop out, but experience had taught her it was a nonissue. She wore a short diaphanous skirt over a scant, shimmery pink triangle scarcely covering her. She wore faux white and pink garters, just for extra props. Her dark hair was flat-ironed and down to her midback, shining with larger bits of pink glitter mixed in.

She felt in charge. The stage was her world, when it was her turn. She willed herself to deafness, having learned the shouts coming from rowdy men made her terribly self-conscious—not great for getting through an act as a naughty fairy. She could, when needed, read the crowd by how many men were standing, waving money, and visibly whooping.

The skirt was the first to go. She raised her arms overhead, the back of her hands touching like a ballerina. She spun to the front of the stage. At the last twirl she unrolled the skirt from her hips, shook her wings to the beat of the loud music, turned around and dropped her ass to the floor. Already, hands were on her, but they were just stuffing the back of her thong. She shook her ass as she slowly stood, hands again over her head. She spun to center stage to her favorite prop, the pole. She had learned to master the pole, to make it her launch pad as she flew around it, wings fluttering, legs splitting apart and wrapping around the pole, and a backbend to make a contortionist stop and stare. When she landed, she lit gently on her heels, fell gracefully to the floor and crawled on all fours to the front with a mischievous look on her face. Men greedily pushed past one another to shove bills into her cleavage and thong.

The garters went second, with her performing a graceful balancing act and bending forward, ass to audience for the finish. Occasionally a man or two would be too drunk or high to have the sense to stay off the stage, but two big men would grab them before they made it to their feet.

For her finale, she lost her wings, the end of her innocence. She spun to the front and pouted, turning from side to side like a little girl caught being naughty. Slowly she unhooked her bra and the wings dropped to the floor. Her freed breasts bounced a bit but then stayed at attention, plump and perky, nipples erect. She posed with her hands on hips, taking in the lewd smiles, fluttering bills, and gaping mouths. Then she strutted around the stage, her breasts bouncing along with her. Back to the front, licking her fingers, she would rub her nipples slowly, before falling to her knees and fake-humping/riding the stage. Then she straddled the stage, balancing herself with her arms in back so that her tiny pink triangle and what it barely covered greeted the men. Bills were shoved into her thong straps; she removed them to make room for others. New music signaled the end of her set. She righted herself, collected her bills, strutted toward the curtain and blew the audience a kiss.

Inevitably, Veronika would be in the wings, waiting to hug and praise her, despite that she was not next in line—Miss Kitten, the scandalous teacher was next. Her hug was welcome, because Laney's performance high would inevitably be wearing off, and she had to brace herself for the crash, sometimes vomiting from some unidentifiable ickiness flowing relentlessly through her bloodstream.

No, no. She could not let Jeff, or anyone else, get inside of her head. Her mind and body were her own. It was no wonder, though, that Debbie seemed to dislike Laney since her first day on the job. God knew how much staring at her ass Jeff engaged in when Laney was unaware.

Why did intimidating men have to be on her review committees?

In addition to lascivious Jeff, there was Dante Michaels, the chair of the African diaspora department. When certain Black colleagues, including him, were in the room, she never felt quite culturally "authentic" enough. It was an imposter syndrome of a different sort. Her research felt too removed from the concerns of African Americans, she wasn't enough involved in the lives of Black students, she didn't always show up at functions showcasing Africana themes, and so forth. None of this could be written against her in any serious review, but it could certainly color his, and others', opinions of her.

Take Dante's work on the Black family. He postulated that the African-American family unit was the source of critical political capital. That was obviously tied to the concerns of Black Americans. Furthermore, it indicated his belief that Black relationships were an important foundation for social success. It wasn't easy to dismiss such observations. It wasn't easy to not give a damn about his perspectives.

She hated that she had to be concerned with what others thought, but it was part of the serious hazing process that could lead to exclusive membership in the job security club. Job security—tenure—would be a momentous historical event for a member of the Travers clan, at least since the 1940s, when her, great-great-grandmother owned a bustling hair salon business, and her great-great-grandfather did pretty well on his own with a well-placed shoeshine station. Been a long time since the '40s.

Laney sighed as she searched for more staples and letterhead. Such was the occupation she signed up for.

Chapter Eight

TIE'S MOOD WAS sour, despite that he would soon be dining with Laney. The difficulty was that they would be joined by Gaston Stokely, his studio guest from this evening's show. Gaston had been on for only eight minutes, but back in Chicago, Tie had a habit of taking any studio guest out to dinner when they could spare the time. He planned to occasionally invite Laney along, as he thought she might be intrigued by some of his guests. And the fact that she was a charming, knowledgeable conversationalist didn't hurt.

But Gaston had a grating personality. Rather than sensibly allowing Tie to drive them both to the restaurant, Gaston insisted on driving them both in his top-of-the-line Mercedes S-class. He wouldn't even hear of them driving separately, waving away logic. "It's such a luxury to drive this baby," he said. "Otherwise, it's too frustrating in the city, even this little town. Have to have a driver take you everywhere."

Of course. How inconvenient. So he was forced to endure the car ride.

Gaston tossed his keys to the valet outside of the restaurant—this after insisting that they patronize this place where he knew the chef—and put his arm around Tie's shoulder as if they were the best of buddies. "Ain't she a beaut?"

Tie assumed he meant the car.

He was relieved to see Laney already seated at one of the front booths. He kissed her on the cheek, made introductions, and tucked himself in beside her.

He hadn't been to this establishment, Fleur, before. But as soon as they were seated, he understood the name of the place. Beautiful unique flower centerpieces were at each white cloth covered table, and the dark wood paneling seemed to make all the colors pop. He noticed that all of the menus were different, too, with a different reprint of a famous painting or sketch of flowers on each booklet. The couple next to them dined on salads that—he had to look twice—had flower petals in them.

Gaston was looking at him, smiling. "Huh? Huh? Ain't it great? Gasteau, that's the chef, is trying to bring back the use of flowers as essential part of cuisine, both as ambience and as embellishment and flavor. With all the talk about phytochemicals and whatnot these days, he's onto something." He shrugged. "Some folks think it's hackneyed and tone deaf, but I think Gasteau is a genius."

Of course. Gaston and Gasteau. Tie wouldn't have been surprised to learn that they were the same person.

"Certainly interesting. I was just flipping through the menu before you two arrived."

Gaston's attention lingered on Laney. Finally he turned to Tie. "She's beautiful. Very exotic."

Tie looked at Laney, mortified, and admired the Mona Lisa smile she maintained on her face. Surely, she knew he wouldn't respond with something so inane as "Thanks! She's mine!" but he figured she had also been rendered speechless herself, although she was hiding it well. Tie put his hand atop hers, which was in her lap.

"Soooooooooo," Gaston began, breaking the silence.

Tie picked up his wineglass.

"You've been at *Biz-E Life* evening for two, three years now."

Tie saw fit to do nothing but nod so he could drink.

"I hadn't heard what you'd been doing before then. You were like AWOL there for a good while, weren't you?"

"Not to folks who knew me, journalism, or radio."

"Don't you ever wonder what more education could have done for you, man?"

"Not at all." Tie lied. "The college education I had under my belt gave me the basics to understand what seem like the most complicated processes in our economic landscape—but you and I know it's not that deep. I like to think it helps me talk in lay terms with laypeople."

"Ah, the people," King Gaston said.

"So, I've been working my way up the ranks at WLAK in Chicago, which happened to be the home station for *Biz-E Life*. That was after some time at KQED. Nothing magical. No obligatory years in corporate, so my soul is intact. Not so much to tell."

Gaston picked up his bourbon and sipped. "Hmmph. Not so much like father, like son, huh?"

Tie gripped his wineglass. "Not so much."

His hand was still atop Laney's, and the soft skin of her

other hand now caressed his.

"Wish I could have gotten away with that. No—take that back, because then I wouldn't have my S-class or my two houses!"

"Heaven forbid," Tie mumbled into his wine.

He wasn't hungry enough to try out the chrysanthemum petals in his salad when it was brought out to him.

"Aw, come on. Be a good sport."

"I'm an excellent sport. I'm just not hungry for salad."

"Believe it or not, flowers and greens are excellent palate cleansers."

Tie looked around.

"Seriously, though, Tie, why didn't you finish your education, get a PhD, man?"

"Gaston, what scholarship are you involved in now that makes you so knowledgeable about tariffs? I heard your fascinating interview with Tie this evening." Tie couldn't tell from the slight edge in Laney's voice whether she'd had enough of Gaston's pestering and showboating or whether she was truly just bored to death with their dinner companion. She pushed greens around on her plate.

Gaston turned to Laney and winked. "I know a lot about a lot of things, sweetie. But I track tariffs like poor people track lottery numbers." He went on to fill Laney in on how he came to be brilliant on yet another subject, and Tie took the moment to collect his thoughts.

He didn't like the feeling that he was using Laney to deal with this guy as a way to divert attention from uncomfortable subjects. Laney had better things to do. And the guy was treating Laney like a little girl. He couldn't let Gaston intimidate him. Not tonight. Not anymore.

Gaston paused in his soliloquy long enough to place a sizable portion of crab cake in his mouth. "You know, Gaston, Laney teaches at Sheffield College just outside of the city. She's doing some pretty important scholarship herself."

Laney nodded. If Gaston had a civil bone in his body, this was the chance to prove it.

But Gaston barely nodded.

"Neat," he said before stuffing more crab cake into his mouth. He turned back to Tie. "You must get shit from your father for your questionable choices, though, right? Something along the lines of 'those who can't teach...'" Gaston laughed. "Not that you're not a great teacher. My colleagues come in laughing at your program lines on a daily basis."

Tie ignored the buried insult. "My father's a professor. Laney's a professor. That's real teaching, and that I can't fathom."

"Yeah, but he's an *expert*. Isn't that something you wouldn't mind having? Marketable expertise?"

"Who says I don't have expertise?" Tie tapped his plate with his fork, ignoring the annoyed looks of those seated next to them.

He didn't look in Laney's direction. Whatever her feelings at the moment, they would not be pleasant to witness. He wouldn't stand to see pity in her eyes, and he couldn't bear to see her suppressing anger. He had to get them out of there.

"I actually have to get going early tomorrow. Usually

there's no big rush into the office, but I'm often on other folks' schedules. Ben Bernanke needs to interview early."

"Patience. You know I was actually on the medium list for his former position?"

"The medium list?"

"Well, before the short list. The point is, I'm in with the White House now as a frequent financial consultant. Not the same name recognition as your father, but up there."

Tie looked at the sea bass now placed before him. It smelled delicious, but... "They put little nasturtiums where the eyes would have been?"

"Genius, right?"

"A little macabre for my taste. Makes me feel like I'm eating some poor fish's newly deceased spouse."

Gaston gestured at Tie's phone on the table. "You got any pictures of them?" He licked some panko crumbs from his lips.

"Who?"

"Oh, come on, Stevens. When were you ever without some hot chicks at your side?"

Tie refused to consider Laney a hot chick, and felt ill at the thought of this idiot drooling over her, but he would at least point out the obvious.

"There's no them, and there are certainly no chicks. I'm with Laney, Dr. Travers. I don't have pictures of random women in my phone—come on, Gaston. This isn't college."

Gaston seemed dubious but let it go. He was on his second bourbon and apparently was a lightweight, despite his obese status. "In addition to my fat six figures, I'm playing the market so well that I'm actually worth seven. Plus, I don't limit my career pursuits to just one thing. I've got corporate as my wife, and consulting and commissioned analysis as pieces of side ass." He bellowed with laughter again. "Hey, I can hook you up if you ever get tired of the little media thing."

Laney drew in a sharp intake of breath.

Tie's ears grew hot and his jaw tightened. "Thanks, but I don't see leaving 'the media thing' anytime soon. I've won a couple of awards on my reporting and the show. And I fit comfortably within my own six figures—"

"I know. I googled your income." Gaston looked proud.

Tie pretended not to hear him. "Not including all my investments, although I can't pretend I'm anywhere nearing seven. I don't need it. I'm happy."

"Awards, huh?" Gaston started in on his third drink. "You always had awards for something or other. Tennis trophies, debate club ribbons. But it's a shame those things don't get you into the upper echelon." He finally turned toward Laney again. "What about you, sugar? Is our media star over here making enough money to keep you happy?"

She set her fork down with much clatter. "We are quite happy, thanks. I actually have my own income—they pay women these days. And for god's sake, don't call me sugar, sweetie, or any other name besides Dr. Travers."

Gaston looked startled, confused, then laughed nervously. "A bit of a spitfire you've got here, Tie. Sure she's not too much for you?"

Tie had enough of his bass. It tasted good, but the fish-filled table was beginning to reek.

Laney wasn't finished. "I'll tell you who's too much."

"Look, I hate to rush you, Gaston," Tie jumped in quickly.

He did not need Laney fighting his battles for him. It wasn't fair to her and, frankly, it was humiliating to him. He looked at his watch.

"Oh, I should really get you a Rolex. Maybe as a thank-you gift for the interview." He winked.

"No, I like my watch, and it's my job to thank you." Tie quickly signed the receipt for dinner, smiled widely and stood, extending a hand to a sour-looking Laney.

Gaston, finishing his drink as quickly as possible, had no choice but to follow. "That waitress was hot, wasn't she?" He winked at Tie.

"I should probably drive you… to a hotel."

"The hell you will. I'm possessive about my wheels. And I am not drunk. I drove here from New York and I'll be going back that same way. I have no desire to stay overnight in Columbus, Ohio."

"Well, it is late…"

"So I'll stop somewhere on the way." Gaston was gruff and sulked during the walk to the parking lot. Tie was doubly grateful that Laney was here, as she could take him back to the studio to get his car, preventing any further excruciating moments with Gaston.

They sat silently in Laney's car watching the Mercedes tear out of the lot. Tie was too embarrassed to say anything, and Laney was probably playing it safe. Would they often have to endure these awkward moments?

Gaston had all but come out and pointed out the fact that Tie didn't have his college degree. Tie's stomach had knotted every time Gaston mentioned education. He couldn't proceed like this around Laney. Weren't they trying to get to know each other, warts and all? He certainly didn't want her to think he'd falsely presented himself somehow, especially if they got around to having sex again.

"Laney."

She looked at him with a mix of emotions reflected in her eyes.

"There's something I... haven't made clear to you. It's about my education." He turned to her fully.

Now the look in her eyes was curiosity.

"I... haven't attained my college degree. I did go to Wisconsin, stayed nearly three years, but then decided that school learning was not necessarily leading me down the path I wanted to take." He rambled, afraid to give her a chance to react.

He paused, not knowing what more to say. He searched her eyes for her reaction. Her eyes shined as always, and the curiosity remained.

"Wow. You got all the way to where you are without having graduated college? That amazes me! I'm impressed actually. How... how..."

"How did I do it? Luck was on my side."

"And I've told you, you also have the talent."

He smiled. "I told you, it all pretty much started with an internship and I worked my way up from there. And observing and reading. Lots and lots of reading."

She stared at him; she really did seem to be in awe.

"I'll admit that I was afraid to tell you, because... I didn't want you to think any less of me. But now... I don't think I have to worry about that."

She nodded. "I don't care about pedigree, baby. Never even occurred to me. You could hold your own around anyone in my circle. No worries. And I'm still attracted to you like you wouldn't believe." She touched the side of his face. He leaned over and kissed her.

Tie's relief was almost palpable. He was sure Laney must have felt the breeze of the burden drifting from his shoulders.

She started the car and he smiled. The evening was ending on a more positive note than he'd anticipated.

Chapter Nine

To his relief, Tie's on-site producer, Jason, was as friendly and accommodating as Blue. Though Tie could work with any number of personalities, his preference was for those who came without complications. Cheryl, the station manager, was very enthusiastic about Tie's arrival and did what she could to make his transition as seamless as possible. He had been relieved no one had to give up their office to accommodate his presence. He wanted to disrupt the flow as little as possible.

He quickly became familiar with some of the local programming and was impressed with the station's offerings. The staff had put a lot of work into diversifying their programming as much as possible. They even broadcast a show focused on LGBTQ concerns, and its host was one of the liveliest characters Tie had ever met. Yes, he'd landed in a good place. *So quit opposing and grousing about this move, Craig, buddy. I'm not going to turn into a country bumpkin.*

Indeed, if he had spare time, he would discover Columbus's admirable arts and culture scene. He and Laney hadn't managed to take advantage of any of this scene so far, but he looked forward to doing so.

As predicted, however, planning the fundraiser was consuming much of his time. Through his job, Laney's, and the connections of other people, he was able to recruit enough volunteers for Skylar, his impressive event planner, to form the necessary planning committees and subcommittees. It wasn't cheap, but he was funding most of the event out of pocket. He was convinced it would pay off outrageously in the future, as national financial literacy programs would make a significant dent in student debt. He also had faith that they would reach his ninety-five-thousand-dollar fundraising goal, although identifying wealthy donors was the area he was falling behind in. But not for long. There wasn't time for delay.

"TIE!" LANEY THREW her arms around his neck and inhaled his intoxicating scent and relished in the exhilaration of his touch. "What a handsome sight for sore eyes!" She glanced at the silver clock on the wall. "This is actually great timing. I was considering whether to go outside for lunch or to sit in front of my laptop as usual, with a cup of noodles."

His hands were clasped behind the small of her back. "Nah. We can't have that. I'm glad I came to your rescue."

Suddenly she pulled away. "I forgot my door is open." As comfortable as she felt with Tie, she was still uncomfortable with the prospect of adding fuel to the stories students were likely exchanging concerning her relationship with him.

"We were being good."

"Oh, we were being very tame, by our standards," she

whispered. "But not the point." She drummed her fingers on her desk. "Where should we go? Actually, I don't have a whole lot of time, so let's stay on campus. The options aren't too bad."

They walked over toward the student center, which was in the same traditional early nineteenth century building style as the rest of the quaint campus. True to its name, many students occupied the space, but Laney was at ease in presenting herself and Tie as friends. Tie seemed a little nervous and kept looking at her hand, but she tried to ignore it, her heart tightening a little with sympathy. Trees lined the walkways, so there was no shortage of gold, crimson, molten orange and amber leaves to kick their way through. She laughed as she kicked some leaves his way. She was truly happy to see him, and she wanted to interact with him playfully, if not sensually.

She led him to one of her favorite spots on campus, a buffet area downstairs, where patrons paid by the pound. She quickly gave Tie the scoop and a standing tour, and they went about making their selections. She was in front of the burrito bar when Ken Davis sidled up to her.

She glanced at him. "Hey, Ken."

"Laney." He continued standing beside her, unmoving.

Okay, now what? She looked up at him again and studied the strange expression on his hard face. It seemed partly condescending and part… something she couldn't identify.

"Surely you're not too good for a brother."

Laney's mouth dropped open. *What? What the hell is this about?* Her mind spun and she couldn't think of anything to say, so she turned and walked away, feeling squeamish about the exchange. She didn't bother continuing to fill her plate because she'd lost her appetite, her stomach shrank to the size of a walnut. She noted where Ken sat down—at a table full of some of her Black male colleagues. Was Dante Michaels there? Yup, yup, yup. Her breath quickened. All of them together. And here she was with Tie, who was by all appearances not Black. She sipped her water but couldn't take a bite of the salad she'd managed to get.

Tie finally sat across from her, his plate full mostly of California rolls. He gave Laney one look and his face paled. She turned away from him and again looked at her Black colleagues. Was anyone staring at them?

"What's wrong?"

She looked at him, worry clouding her thoughts. "N-nothing. Okay, it's not nothing." Should she even go there with Tie? Would he understand? Well, there was only one way to find out. And this situation seemed to speak for itself. She leaned toward him, whispering, "Ken, that guy over there"—she nodded toward the faculty-filled table—"the one wearing the plaid jacket, he came up to me at the buffet. Didn't you see him?"

"No."

"Well, he came up to me and said, kind of under his breath, 'Surely you're not too good for a brother.' Yes, he said that!"

She expected him to look surprised or outraged, but he only looked confused. Did he not know what "brother" meant? Oh, this was so hard! She felt angry about the situation but also frustrated and worried.

She started to see some sympathy in his eyes, but there was still the curiosity. Both emotions had his forehead crinkled and she wondered what he was thinking. He opened his mouth to speak, closed, it, then opened it again a few seconds later. "That sounds very rude, not to mention like nonsense. Do you think he was just trying to make a joke?"

No. Tie hadn't seen Ken's hard eyes. It was no joke. There was nothing remotely funny about it. "Even if that's the case, it's hitting below the belt. I didn't answer him; I was stunned."

"What is worrying you about it?"

She licked her lips and glanced at the table full of faculty again. "Undoubtedly, he repeated his words to the other men at the table. They've been sending some dismissive glances this way, instead of the usual polite head nod. Not all of them, just a couple. Not Dante Michaels, thank goodness. He's on my tenure committee. Still, enough to make me nervous." She pushed her salad plate away. "I'm definitely not hungry. In fact, can we leave? I'm sorry."

Laney did not wait for his response but left the table and came back with some Styrofoam boxes, handing one to Tie. This was unfair to poor Tie. He didn't get it. And she wouldn't be able to make him see. But she wasn't going to prolong the discomfort.

"The college is very slow in moving toward an environmentally friendly place," she said absentmindedly, referring to the Styrofoam.

Tie spilled a little of his food in the rush to keep up with her. He wasn't angry; he just seemed concerned. She was sure he had questions about this circumstance. She led him out of the eating nook, nodding at the men, most of whom were turned in her direction. She waited until she and Tie were out of the building before she took a deep breath. She needed to think. She needed to figure things out.

"Where are you parked?" She turned to him.

He looked shocked. "In the lot by your building, of course. But don't you still have time left? We can walk and talk a bit more or close the door to your office and—"

"I really need time to process, Tie. I'm sorry." Her throat began to close. "I'm sorry lunch was ruined. I just have to figure out what's going on." She looked down at her Born boots.

He sighed. "Well, at least I got a hug from you... before being dismissed."

Her head shot up at his words and she shook her head. He looked so dejected, something she hadn't anticipated.

She put her hand on his arm, and looked directly into his dimmed eyes. "I'm not trying to dismiss you, honey. I just need to think things through. I'll be too preoccupied to be good company, anyway." It was true. She probably wouldn't do too well in the classroom, either. Oh, why couldn't these things roll off her back?

"I'm not sure why you can't figure things out with me. I can help. Be a sounding board."

Laney had not considered that. But it would be too difficult for him, probably. How could he relate? He had looked so confused.

"I don't know. Maybe not in this situation. Just, just, please, give me the space and I'm sure I'll have my head together later."

Tie shrugged, looking down. He finally looked up, leaned forward to kiss her, but then stopped, looking around. "Goodbye, Laney."

Her heart sank as she watched him walk away.

Oh, why couldn't she have been content with her cup of noodles?

Chapter Ten

D URING THE NEXT week, things were starting to ramp up at work for Laney, with committee work getting impossibly unwieldy and advisees starting to lose their minds about their workload. It was all she could do to somehow manage to prepare for and successfully teach. Never mind write up any of the research she'd accomplished over the summer.

She had managed to avoid seeing Tie, coming up with weak excuses related to work. She wasn't ready to face him yet, not having sorted out her feelings about being with him in public—at least, on campus. For that matter, her feelings about dating a White man, period.

During one particularly rushed day, Laney sat across from Tracey at one of the cafes on campus. The problem with having lunch, or any public conversation, on campus was that, unless she wanted her business broadcasted soon after, she had to very carefully scan who was in the listening radius. And some of their colleagues seemed to have super-sonic hearing and ninja stealth. Debbie being only one. Some of her colleagues really needed to get lives.

"So," Laney got right to it. "The man who was responsible for my 'new glowing complexion,' I think you'd said a few weeks ago, he's back in my life."

Tracey's eyes widened and she clasped her hands together. "Oh, girl, tell."

Laney's face warmed. "Not much to tell. Boy meets girl. Boy falls for girl. Girl falls for boy. Boy falls off the face of the earth, then from the sky. Anyway," she said at Tracey's confused expression, "we're taking it slowly, you know."

Tracey leaned in. "And, I take it, he's not one of ours?" she whispered.

Laney wasn't sure how to respond.

With Tracey, she had no problem telling it either way. "No…" she said. "He's not a Sheffield colleague. No thank you there."

"Yeah, I'm your what-not-to-do case in that regard. Take your ass to the library if you want to learn Black studies, Mr. English-Lit Professor. Don't bore me to death with your pressing questions." She rolled her eyes and Laney chuckled.

"Well, and he's not one of ours in that sense, either."

"Oh… you mean he's going to be asking you what it's like to be the only Black person in a room and all that jazz?"

"No, hasn't so far. And no apparent jungle fever. Yet."

"You're expecting him to eventually reveal that he just wanted to experience sex with a Black woman?"

"No, not expecting, but I won't be oblivious, either. The last time I dated a White guy—which has only been once before, and that lasted two days—I asked up front whether he had some sort of jungle fever thing going. Some primitive attraction to Black women, all physical. I can't mess around with that nonsense. But I haven't directly asked Tie."

"Shoot, I could deal with it, for the right guy!" Tracey was killing her Caesar salad.

"Anyway. Back to Tie. I'm pretty sure we're okay on the jungle fever front, although I've had so many men trying to collect their 'black card' through me, I'm still on guard. And I get a little self-conscious, especially around our brothers and sisters."

"Though few and far between they are."

"For instance, the other day when Tie and I were eating at the center, Ken implied that I think I'm too good for a Black man. I kid you not!"

"For real? Wow. He's such an asshole, though. You know he had to say something. I wouldn't go anywhere with it."

"But that made me a lot more hesitant about being with Tie. First there's the question of whether he is exoticizing me, and then there's this." She leaned back and threw her hands in the air. "But I love being with him... we have this inexplicable, powerful attraction. And I haven't been treated so well by a man in... well, I don't know! Anyway, I haven't come right out and told him that we need to stop seeing each other, but... come on, you know there's a renewed move-ment, especially among Black women, that's pushing against our dating outside of the race. Gotta date Black men. Gotta support *our* men."

"Well, that's some Black women. I'd wager not the ma-jority." Tracey put down her fork. "Do you actually hear yourself? You just implied that he's treated you better than any man has before. Why the hell are you looking for problems?"

"But I still feel very torn, to be honest. And guilty. I can't shake the feeling that I'm doing something wrong. Especially as a professor and as a role model."

"I hear you, but these aren't the people who are going to keep you warm at night. Try not to stay in your head too much, Professor."

Laney rolled her eyes. "Anyway. Perhaps the more important detail of interest to you is his minor celebrity-dom."

Tracey pushed her salad away and folded her hands in front of her. "Do. Freakin'. Tell."

LATER THAT DAY, Nette and Laney were sitting in the Whole Foods café for a light dinner, despite Laney's protests at having to leave her house. She had too many papers to grade and she would have to talk about Tie, which she had done enough of for the day. Not that any of this mattered. Nette essentially ordered her out of the house.

Now Nette wasted no time diving into her mint and couscous salad. "I'm going to eat," she mumbled between forkfuls. "So you have to talk. Tell me what's going on with Tie. From what you told me earlier, it sounds like you've been avoiding him all week. He was your prince. What the hell happened?"

"So, I don't get to eat?" Laney asked guardedly, despite the fact she had no appetite for her turkey and cranberry relish sandwich—or anything else for that matter.

"You'll have your chance."

"He was a prince in the one-night stand narrative. We weren't supposed to pursue a relationship, which complicates things. But we're trying to, so, well, it's complicated. But it's not about Tie. It's me."

"Oh boy... that sounds like a breakup line."

"Well, I'm just having trouble getting past the race thing. On one hand it seems hopeless, but—"

Nette's fork froze in the air. "What race thing? What are you talking about?"

"Oh—I guess I haven't really told you. It's just... you know, the whole interracial dating thing and the challenges that go with it."

Nette put her fork down. "No, I don't know. Since when do you have a problem with interracial anything? Your best friend is White. Or at least, I thought I was your best friend."

"No, you're not understanding—and that's one of the problems. It's different with dating, Nette." Laney picked at her bread and looked out the window, not seeing.

"Well, I've dated Black men. I haven't noticed much difference."

"Nette, you think you're Black in the first place."

"You need to stop saying that. It's offensive. And untrue."

Laney had crossed a line. She hadn't wanted to bring up race, but it was an integral part of why she was hesitant to see Tie again. She remained silent.

"So, I've dated Black men as a *White woman* and I've

certainly never had a problem with it."

Laney didn't know how to respond. As woke as she found Nette to be, some things were just bound to be lost in translation. But her friend had a point—she was Laney's best friend. Obviously, race didn't factor into the intimacy of their relationship. Why should it be different for dating and romantic relationships? Because of what it *looked* like? To people like Ken and Dante? She suddenly realized she hadn't really been concerned with "keeping up appearances" until these last couple of years on the tenure track. If there was any selling out taking place... maybe it was herself.

Nette shifted in her seat and picked up her fork. "Well. Um. I guess you should know that I broke up with Devin. So I guess I can't pass too much judgment."

Laney turned back to Nette, resting her hand on her friend's side of the table. "Nette, I'm so sorry. He seemed really special."

"Whatever. It's my fault. I should have known better than to say the L-word. I had too much wine last night or something, dammit. But what's done is done. We can drop it."

"Oh, yes, you loved him." Laney felt her friend's loss.

Nette sighed. "You know I don't think it wise to tell someone you love them before you've seen them on the toilet, unpolished in the morning, and at their angriest."

"How efficient if you can catch all three in one fell swoop," Laney replied wryly.

"It was stupid of me, okay? End of subject."

"He didn't break up with you. You broke up with him

because you told him that you loved him!"

"Again, I have rules."

"Listen, Nette, you've broken every other of your rules with this guy so far, what's so sacred about this one?"

"What's so sacred about proclaiming one's love? Please, Laney."

Laney scrunched her brow. "I'm pretty sure I asked *you* that, my germaphobic friend. What is it about love that freaks you out more than germs?"

"Can we drop it? I'm not a psychologist like your highness, but I can tell you're trying at all costs to divert the subject from you and Tie." Nette stopped munching, and looked at Laney with angry eyes. "So? Is there some metaphorical meaning you can pull from my toilet rule? With regard to you and Tie?"

"Besides the very basic conclusion that your toilet is full of shit?"

Nette gave her a death-ray stare from her gray eyes. "Forget it. I didn't realize you're a relationship expert." Nette picked up her cell phone and started looking at apps, which was her way of saying "get the fuck gone."

Great.

She wrapped her sandwich in napkins and left the table, with a last look at her best friend. Nette didn't return her gaze.

Chapter Eleven

TIE WAS PLEASANTLY surprised when Laney answered her phone. Somehow, they had gone all week without talking. She hadn't returned his calls except when he was on the air, which he found suspicious. She had been sending him brief text messages, but that wasn't satisfactory. He kept trying to assure himself it was due to her busyness rather than intended avoidance, but given their last encounter, he couldn't maintain optimism.

"Tie." Her voice was such a welcome sound.

"Laney. I've been trying to reach you, honey, but somehow we haven't been connecting."

Laney was silent.

"Is there something you want to tell me?"

"No, no. I've just been busy—and preoccupied. I've missed you. I'm sorry I've been hard to get ahold of."

"Will I see you sometime soon?"

Laney was silent.

"Laney?"

"I'm here. I was just thinking through my schedule. Of course we'll be able to see each other soon. I should be free on Saturday."

The conversation was the most awkward they'd ever had.

Something was off.

"We should probably talk about what happened the other day. You were pretty upset, and that's been bothering me since."

"Uh…we will. At a later time, okay? I'm at the office now and have to rush to class soon."

Another convenient excuse to avoid talking.

"Okay, honey."

He hung up the phone feeling even less optimistic. Whatever was eating Laney, it was more serious than he'd thought.

AFTER TIE'S BROADCAST, Laney had surprised him by showing up to WYQT not looking so professorial. She wore a blue knit top that hugged her curves nicely and a sexy black skirt with a slit on the side. It was almost too much. There were only so many things one could do while trying to avoid full-blown sex with his girlfriend. Still, she had allowed him to go to third base with her, caressing her below the waist and between her incredible thighs, and he managed to maintain self-control. They hadn't even made it out to the car, so he was glad that the floor was mostly empty. He was too happy—and relieved—to see her again to rock the boat by not controlling his desire for her. It helped to see that she was struggling with passion just as much. Hot blood coursing through both their touching bodies as they ached for one another. Their kisses made them more and more delirious.

They would soon have to revisit this "no sex" agreement. But, for now, Tie was more than satisfied. Too satisfied to mention the awkward phone call from earlier. Whatever spurred her to pull this surprise visit, he wanted to show his appreciation.

Later, as they walked hand in hand down the Scioto mile, they paused to look at the moon's broken white reflection in the inky water. Despite being in the city center, the effect was of feeling like they were the only two people around.

He looked at her profile, admired her long lashes directed toward the water. A breeze blew her curls away from her neck and he wanted to kiss her exposed skin.

"What?" She turned to him.

"I was just thinking, wondering where this marvelous woman came from. I don't know much about your family. You alluded to your sister having some addiction troubles, but that's it."

Laney turned back toward the river. "There's really not much to say. It was just me, Lola and my mother. My parents emigrated from Jamaica before we were born. Our father left when I was a toddler, and my mother never spoke of him. Lola's just a year older than me, so she doesn't remember anything, either. At least, nothing that she's ever shared with me. My mother was depressed most of the time. We grew up in our own bubbles."

"I'm sorry to hear that."

"Don't be. Apparently we didn't need him in order to survive." She paused and seemed to be considering something. "And, my mother died a few years ago from cancer," she finally added.

"Gosh, I'm so sorry to hear this, Laney." He put his arm around her and rubbed her arm.

"Don't be. She lived her life as fully as she was ever going to live it."

There was a long pause.

"I guess I underestimate how fortunate I was to have the old man around." Tie glanced at her and thought relief crossed her face. Talking about family must have been hard for her. So he continued with the change of subject. "As inferior as he made me feel, I do believe he loves me, although I sure didn't back then." He paused. "Just believe he would have loved me more if I had the highest grades in school and more trophies on the wall. I guess with being adopted, after your parents' first child was born with intellectual disabilities, a lot of stock gets placed in you. You catch a lot of shit for not being the dream your parents had. I actually thought he detested me and couldn't wait until I went to college, out of his sight. Some of that might have been true. He could have loved me and detested me at the same time."

Laney looked surprised. "Meg has intellectual disabilities?"

Tie shrugged. "Yeah. She was born with Down syndrome. I guess that wouldn't necessarily have come up unless you met her."

Laney put her arm around his waist. "Well, I wish your mother had come to your defense. You deserved praise, not criticism." She kissed the cleft on his chin. "Still do." Her words lifted his spirit and lit something within his chest. These were the times when he almost felt confident that she was not ashamed to be with him.

He turned toward her. "But being around you often makes me feel like a better person, like my best might just be good enough, somehow."

Laney turned to him and threw her arms around his neck, effectively ending the discussion. As his head bent toward hers, he relished the natural kiss they shared. Laney's full lips were soft and irresistible. It all felt so right. Surely they were made for each other.

Chapter Twelve

THE NEXT MORNING, Laney stared at the invitation, wondering if it would change with maybe the fourth reading. Randy Wilkins, in the African diaspora department, had sent an invitation to faculty members of color, a chance to socialize, greet, and meet. Kind of late in the semester but typical. The invitation encouraged recipients to "bring your significant other! Come join the family."

Tie counted as her significant other, but she hesitated. Would Dante Michaels be there? What would he think? Would that asshole Ken be there, rocking her boat again? But as Tracey had put it, what did it matter what others thought? And perhaps Nette's message had gone most directly to Laney's heart. There was obviously no shame in having intimacy with a White person.

Yes. Enough with this nonsense. She would proudly bring Tie to the event. And enjoy it. She wouldn't have thought twice about bringing Dane, her last, dreadlocked, dark-skinned boyfriend, right? Her spirits actually lifted as she RSVPed.

LANEY ALWAYS FELT a bit like an interloper going into Bexley in her Toyota Camry, when most of the parked cars she passed were Audis, BMWs, and Mercedes. That was just the poor child coming out in her, but it still daunted her, and she felt very small. She especially felt the disconnect when she attempted to look elegant, hoping she wouldn't instead come across as an escort. She wished she'd had the money to take all those etiquette classes so she wouldn't have stood out like a sore thumb among her college classmates at Brown. Although there wasn't much etiquette expected in the cafeteria, there were special events and banquets at which anybody in college should have the sense to know which fork to use and when. Though nobody was nasty enough to call her out, she noticed the glances and whispers. Long ago she had become hypervigilant to looks of condescension and the secret conversations among peers.

Anyway, she was heading to Tie's for dinner and felt renewed. No baggage tonight. She drove the unpleasant memories from her mind. She was reminded yesterday evening of the intense connection they shared, physically and emotionally. She was determined to have another lovely night with Tie, being fully "present" for him.

The lobby of Tie's condo building screamed wealth, and she tried to appreciate rather than fear it. The reflection she saw in the elevator doors suggested she could belong there. She did not skimp when it came to dresses.

He greeted her at his door with a very soft kiss, one she suspected would not be representative of the rest of the evening.

"You look… wow. Don't expect me to keep my hands to myself much longer."

"You can get away with it." She winked at him. She knew she looked good. The way the silk red dress complimented her glowing complexion and clung to her curves like a second skin, flaring out at the knees, allowing for a gentle flutter as she walked. And her hair was up, as much as she could manage, with tresses framing her face. She'd tried a new lip color—Heart Crush lip dazzle. And a touch of blush, as Nette had trained her to do. This felt like a special night.

"You look edible, as usual, yourself. But what's behind your back, you trickster?"

"Nothing special." He brought around a bottle of Cristal. "I just want to celebrate. Us. Oh, we'll still have dinner, I promise. But a toast first, to a couple brought together through the airwaves." He popped the cork, allowed for the fizz then poured the light golden liquid into two flutes. "Cheers," he whispered, turning her into jelly with his powerful eyes. Absinthe, she suddenly realized, and immediately wished she hadn't. *Those eyes may be the undoing of me, but I don't dare associate them with the color of a powerful drug.*

"Cheers," she whispered back.

She downed her glass and went to pour another.

"Easy now, I want you to be able to taste my creations." He smiled.

He led her to his dining room with his arm behind her back.

"Wow." She just stood and stared at the beauty before

her, and then gasped when she remembered that he put all of this together.

"You've got real talent, mister! Now…" She strolled around the table. "I assume most of this was catered in, but you probably did the arrangements—they're beautiful, but did you attempt your hand at any of the food, like the soup?" When she received no response, she looked up at him questioningly.

"Are you kidding me, Laney? I go through all this for you and you doubt my talents?" He gestured wildly at the table.

She stared at him, mouth open.

"Yes, my dear, this is all me, and all for you. Well, me too."

"You've got to be…" She glanced at the beautifully pre- pared table again. "You are awesome!"

He turned her to him and took her in a deep kiss that caught her off guard and left her breathless. "You are, too." He turned to the table and pulled out her seat. "Yeah, I took sushi preparation classes back in Chicago. One of the best uses of my time, those classes. I don't do it too often. No point in creating the art when there's no one to enjoy it with you."

"Where on earth did you get cherry blossoms?"

"I have connections." He laughed. "There's a nursery in Hilliard that keeps some plants that somehow defy the season."

He had turned on his electric waterfall, which comple- mented the romantic ambience. The trickling put Laney immediately at peace.

She hesitated before she used her beautiful black-and-gold chopsticks to pick up bright salmon sashimi. He must have sensed her hesitation because he said, "I was trained with a great eye. I use only the freshest, best cuts—yes, even in Columbus, and examine each piece very carefully."

In that case... She closed her eyes and indulged in the buttery texture and mild taste of the sashimi. "Delicious. But so much food, how are we going to eat it all?"

"Don't you worry. Just enjoy." And indeed Laney noticed that he looked at her with intense sensuality as she indulged in his many creations, punctuated here and there by a sip of warm sake.

Afterward, she rubbed her small belly. "Mmmm. You know how to hit it, Mr. Stevens."

He still had that lustful look in his eyes. "Better than sex?"

"Before I met you, I honestly would have said yes. Now, well, obviously you're multi-sensational, but maybe there's something about our synergy, too, huh?"

He scooted closer to her, though he'd been inching closer over the course of dinner. He took her hand and kissed her palm. "Definitely something about our synergy."

As if the gentle kiss on her hand were a false lead, he closed the distance between them and took her mouth voraciously, catching Laney by surprise. She quickly melted into the kiss, and allowed him to begin removing the straps of her dress as he greedily kissed along her neck and then her shoulders. His fingers fiddled with the zipper in her dress and he was visibly frustrated that it went only halfway down her back.

Laney laughed. "There will be no easy sliding out of this one, stud. And as much as I want you, I won't have you ripping it like in some torrid romance novel. This is Versace."

Tie answered by kissing her harder and crushing her to him. She pushed him away to catch a breath and to remove the dress over her head. An appreciative grin spread over his face when he saw that she was bra-less, and standing in a red satin thong. He took in her full, perky breasts and leaned forward to give them his full titillating attention, first caressing them with his large hands then savoring their peaks. Laney brought his head closer to her and enjoyed his tongue for some moments before distancing him enough to unbuckle and unzip his pants and free his very stiff, substantial member. Her delicate hand grasped him and stroked for a few moments. Were they ready to make love again? She still felt some uncertainty about where they were headed, although she felt confident enough that he was not just after a few romps with an exotic woman. And the heat in her core seemed to override any contrary thoughts.

She whispered in his ear, "Shall we head to the bedroom?"

Tie was making his way down to her thong. "Not gonna make it." He panted.

"Oh, Tie." She had to catch her breath. "Not on the table. Everything still looks so beautiful."

"And you would be the piece de resistance." But Tie

grabbed her up by the ass and hoisted her against the dining room wall. His pants fell completely to the floor. He stepped out of them and pushed his briefs down far enough for him to kick them off.

He pressed up against her. "I just can't wait, Laney. I was good all through dinner, watching you savor every bite and wishing I was every fucking piece you put in your mouth. You couldn't really expect me to wait a moment longer. Is this okay, Laney? Should we take the plunge?" His eyes looked desperate.

"Yes. Yes. I'm ready." She barely uttered as he pleasured her, using her own creamy arousal. A moment later she gasped as he fully and quickly entered her, her legs wrapped tightly around him, her three-and-a-half-inch red heels still on her feet.

"Shit, Laney. God didn't mean for us to have anything but bareback sex. You feel so fucking good. So. Damn. Juicy." Tie was pounding into her furiously.

Oh, right. Guess he was too eager to prepare himself. But she certainly didn't want him to stop. She caught their reflection in the mirror on the opposite wall. Tie's perfect ass was clenched. She closed her eyes and moaned, hugging him even deeper into her and not allowing any possibility for this incredible man to slip away.

They later lay on the plush gray dining room carpet, spent and gazing at each other and stroking each other's hair.

"You're so perfect, Laney. You don't know what a gem you are. And how rich I feel."

She gave a small smile. "No, that's supposed to be what I

say."

She wasn't perfect. If she were, she would be fully transparent in the relationship. She would have been more upfront about her racial discomfort. And then maybe it would just be one of those things they dealt with that had some minor interference with their lifestyle, like a severe seafood allergy or vegetarianism. But she suspected it was not that easy.

"Laney…"

She looked at him, realizing that she had drifted off.

"I'm with you, honey." She sat up, scooting toward the wall.

She considered telling him fully about what she had been struggling with. But now was not the time. It had been a beautiful evening and was not yet over.

"You look like you want to tell me something."

"No, it's… you know I always have a million things on my mind. But right now, you have my full attention." She smiled widely.

He pulled himself up next to her and stroked her hair, which had been freed. Gradually but steadily, the kiss that followed developed into the familiar hunger Laney welcomed. Again, Tie hefted her small frame up by her curvy ass and her legs wrapped around his narrow hips. They did not break their kiss until they landed on his bed. Their lovemaking was slow, soft, and less furious, but not lacking the passion of their earlier round.

AFTERWARD, WHILE THEY were lying together and Laney was drawing hearts on his chest, she brought up the faculty of color gathering. Surely, Tie would happily agree to go, given her prior reluctance to have him on campus.

Tie averted his eyes, which had been fastened on her. "That sounds great, baby. But I don't think I'll be able to make it."

Laney propped herself up on her elbow. "Why not?"

He turned his head toward the ceiling. "Um, I think that might be… that could conflict with something I need to do." He chewed on the corner of his lip.

That's a weak excuse. "What do you mean? Either you have a conflict or you don't. If you need to check your calendar, just say that." Her words came out harsher than she'd intended.

He looked back at her. "Okay. I need to check my calendar."

"It would be great if you could come, Tie."

His eyes flashed. "Where is this coming from suddenly? First you don't want me to be on campus and now you want to be around the very people you were avoiding for some reason—at least, in my presence."

Laney took a deep breath and exhaled slowly. "I know. I'm sorry I'm confusing you. But I think I've mostly gotten past the race thing—"

"Race thing?"

She inadvertently held her finger to his lips. "Not to worry about any longer. Let's not talk about it. The point is it would be great for you to meet my colleagues." But relief was not the look she saw reflected in his face. He looked away from her again, but not before Laney saw the worry crinkles between his brows.

"I'll check my calendar."

ON HER WAY home, Laney considered the fact that she had yet to share her concerns with Tie in a more transparent way. Well, he wouldn't understand, would he? And that had not been the point of tonight's visit, anyway. Besides, she felt less anxious about the whole interracial thing, didn't she? After all, she had invited him to a faculty of color gathering.

Which he had not seemed thrilled about. Why was that? She suppressed a fleeting thought, but it bubbled to the surface again. *We finally had sex again. Maybe he got what he wanted. What he's been hanging in here for.*

No. No way. Not Tie. He always seemed interested in her work and what she was engaged in. It had to be something else. Tie was not collecting black cards, for god's sake. But what was it? She sighed. Maybe it was nothing. But she wished that they could get on the same page. They made it together through the "no sex" period. And that was a challenge! But were some challenges just too much?

Chapter Thirteen

O VER THE NEXT few days, Tie continued trying to process their brief discussion about the faculty gathering. It had caught him off guard. He was so accustomed to the thought of Laney wanting him away from campus, for her to invite him to such a function was, of course, a surprise.

Neither had he expected her disappointed reaction. What was she thinking? *I guess my excuse was pretty weak, though.* Well, he couldn't just come right out and say, "No, I'd rather not reveal my lack of education to all your colleagues." Not only would he be embarrassing himself, but he'd also be embarrassing her. Yet she seemed so nonjudgmental about his educational status such worries didn't seem to enter her head.

It was easier and more welcoming to think about planning the fundraiser gala for the youth camp. His event planner, Sky, seemed to be zipping along, so he just needed to work on an invitation list—and leave some seats open for friends of friends. Sky thought they could actually make green, white, and silver work nicely for the event, and it wouldn't be as stifling as black and gold. It worked for Tie. It tied in with his theme, as well as his working name for the program, "All about the Benjamins."

Laney had been enthusiastic about the program since he first told her about it, and jumped in whenever she could to help with planning. This evening, she was going through Sky's notes and indicating her own preferences the planner had narrowed down for venues. For someone who didn't have event planning experience and little familiarity with youth programs, she was making awfully helpful suggestions and contributions. He really owed her.

Tie's leg bounced up and down while he watched Laney at his kitchen table. "You know, baby... I meant to tell you that my schedule is open and I'll be able to attend that faculty event you'd earlier asked me about. Is it too late? Did I miss it?"

Her brown eyes widened. "Really? That would be great! No, you haven't missed it—it's actually this Saturday. Oh, I'm so glad you're coming!" Her smile was wide as she came to throw her arms around his neck and peck him on the lips. He was surprised this meant so much to her. "What changed your mind?"

"My schedule is free."

"Tie..."

He felt his face growing warm. "Look, I see how much time you've sacrificed to try to make this gala work out well. You're doing that for me. I want to make the extra effort when it comes to your events, too."

She gazed at him for a few moments, though he couldn't read her expression. "Well, I appreciate it."

LANEY PARKED HER car on the street near the house bearing the targeted address. The house was practically on campus; they probably could have walked. She looked over at Tie. He was fidgeting a bit in his seat, and his nervousness intensified the butterflies in Laney's own stomach. "Are you okay?" she asked.

"Absolutely! Let's go and get our party on!"

She smiled and the butterflies softened. What was she so worried about? Tie would fit in just fine. This was a progressive, sophisticated group of people, for heaven's sake. The evening would be fine.

Approaching the house, they heard laughter coming from around the back and so they followed the stone path that led around to the backyard. The ivy-draped, white, wooden gate stood open, and Laney led him in.

She stood smiling, on guard for one particular face. She was so focused when she spotted Dante Michaels she was unaware that Randy was walking toward them until he was practically standing in front of her.

"Welcome, Laney! Glad you could make it." He smiled at Tie.

"Oh! Randy, this is Tie Stevens, my… date." Her face was warming. She had never labeled their relationship in public. "Tie, Randy Wilkins. He's the coordinator of this event and… owner of this home?"

They shook hands and Randy nodded. "Well, my partner Nate and I rent from the college, but, yeah, this is our place. Welcome, Tie. Make yourself comfortable. We have a lot of food on the picnic table over there and plenty of drinks—hard and soft. The provost's office is paying, so we've spared no expense!" He gave a hearty laugh and Tie and Laney joined in.

Randy escorted them to the food and pointed out the drinks before excusing himself. "Laney will introduce you around, Tie. She knows everyone," he called over his shoulder.

Laney retrieved a frosty bottle of white wine from a melting bucket of ice and directed Tie to look in one of the coolers for a beer. Drinks in hand, they turned around, and Laney was delighted to see Tracey approaching them.

"You must be Tie," she said, barely looking at Laney. Her hazel eyes gleamed. "I've heard so much about you."

Tie quickly shot Laney a puzzled look but then turned back to Tracey with a smile.

"Yeah, Tie, this is my friend Tracey. I've mentioned her a few times."

Recognition changed his expression and he nodded. "Sounds like Laney owes some of her work sanity to you."

Tracey giggled. Giggled! "The benefits are mutual."

Laney had to suppress a chuckle. She wasn't accustomed to seeing the usual buttoned-up Tracey acting like a schoolgirl.

"So, what's it like being famous?" Tracey asked.

Laney sipped her wine and relaxed. Her gut was right. This evening wouldn't go so badly after all.

AN HOUR LATER, after they both got some food in their stomachs, Tie and Laney were finally alone again. Before Tie had a chance to stop her, Laney whispered, "I'll be right back." She made her way toward a tall woman with long locks and a shorter man standing beside her. He wondered what that was about, but since she didn't exactly invite him, he didn't follow her to find out.

Instead, he sipped his beer. Many couples were present. And a few kids, ranging from about six months to ten years old, he guessed. Most folks were dressed business casual, so he blended in well with his crisp, pale blue shirt and thinly pin-striped dark blue pants. His blue jacket hung on his arm since he'd felt warm the moment they stepped out of the car.

He tried to appear as comfortable as a person standing alone at a social gathering could be. He suddenly registered that he was the only White person present. Mostly African Americans and a few people who looked Latinx, though he couldn't easily tell. Well, this was an unusual experience, although it didn't feel completely unfamiliar.

Two men approached him and shook his hand. He recognized one from the table of men Laney had been preoccupied with a few weeks before. The other man, tall and very attractive, smiled and extended his hand to Tie.

"Reginald Kennedy, from the politics department. And you are?" His thick eyebrows shot up.

Tie happily returned the smile as he shook his hand. "Tie Stevens."

A flicker of recognition crossed Reginald's face and he cocked his head. "No chance you're Tie Stevens from *Biz-E Life*? You said your name almost exactly as he does."

"Yes, the one and only."

"I love your show. I don't have time to read the business news, so it's nice to hear your bite-sized stories when I can catch it. Then I don't have to feel so out of the loop at functions like this!" He laughed heartily. "Oh. This is Ken Davis. Also in politics." He gestured toward his companion.

Ken nodded at Tie. He seemed to be scrutinizing him, the way his eyes narrowed even further when Reginald introduced him.

"Are you new to the college?" Reginald asked.

"No, he's here with Laney." Ken was quick to jump in before Tie even opened his mouth.

"Oh?" A question appeared in Reginald's eyes and his eyebrows shot up again. "Laney's great. As you probably know, she's going up for tenure, and I really wish her the best of luck. I don't think she needs it, though. The luck, that is."

Tie nodded. There was a moment of silence.

"So, Tie, what's your alma mater?" Reginald broke the silence.

Tie gripped his beer a little more tightly. "Uh, Wisconsin." He nodded.

"Oh, good school. Was that undergrad or grad school?"

Tie took a sip of his beer. "Undergrad. I didn't go to graduate school," he quickly added, staving off the predictable next question.

"Oh. Well, on your program you sure sound like you have at least an MBA. You could've fooled me, right, Ken?" He turned to his companion, whose mouth had been hanging open, but he quickly shut it when attention turned to him.

"I actually don't listen to the show. I don't have time." Ken paused. "So, where did you meet Laney? I didn't even know she had any nonacademic friends." His eyes continued to penetrate Tie.

Well, that was a dumb thing to say. Why wouldn't she have nonacademic friends? Friends from college like Nenette, for instance. Though Nenette was a part-timer at the college, she definitely didn't consider herself to be an academic. Tie quickly sized this guy up as a condescending prick. Despite mentally putting him in his place, Tie's face got hot. He hoped he wasn't turning red. He did not care to let people know when they were riling him.

"I met her at my talk and book signing. My new book, which, incidentally, has an academic publisher. Perhaps you find that ironic?"

Reginald chuckled. "Well, academic or not, you're a professor through the airwaves. So I'm sure you don't have much spare time—none of us do—but I always wondered whether you had a consulting business on the side or something."

As Tie focused on Reginald, Ken's eyes bored into him. "No, not yet, though I'm considering it. Right now I have my mind wrapped around a program I'm trying to develop to promote financial literacy in underrepresented youth."

Reginald's face grew thoughtful. "That certainly sounds like a worthwhile program. You know who's really tapped into the funding opportunities for youth programs? Melinda Hogan, in sociology. Did you know that?" He turned to Ken. Ken's lips were tight as he shook his head.

"Speak of the—" Reginald tapped on the arm of a woman who was walking by with a plate of cheese and crackers and a glass of wine. "Mel! I was just mentioning you to Tie here. Tie Stevens, this is Mel Hogan."

"Pleasure to meet you." Tie nodded at her, sparing her the need to awkwardly balance the plate and glass for a handshake.

"Pleasure's mine. To what do I owe the mention?"

"I was just telling him about your funding connections. He's developing a youth program to promote financial literacy."

Mel's forehead crinkled as her eyes widened. "Oh? Do tell! I'm actually sitting at one of the tables over there. Why don't you join us?" She indicated a table seated by a woman and two men.

Tie's head swiveled to look for Laney.

Reginald put his hand on Tie's back. "If I see Laney, I'll steer her toward you." He smiled. "Nice meeting you. Enjoy the party." He and Ken left, the other not having spoken a word since Tie's last to him.

Tie turned to Mel. "Great. Thanks, I appreciate you taking the time to discuss this with me."

"I'll introduce you to some other folks who are better at associating with donors with deep pockets. Yeah, we have a lot to talk about." She laughed lightly as they walked toward the white cloth-covered table.

Tie breathed a sigh of relief. Maybe he could get through the rest of the evening without his competence and suitability for Laney being questioned.

"THANK YOU, BABY. I'm really glad I decided to attend this event with you."

"You mean you're glad your schedule opened up?" She winked at him, and his face heated a little. She chuckled as she turned on the ignition.

"In *any* case, it was well worth my time. Everyone was great. I made a number of contacts, and I mean really useful contacts for getting this program started. Beyond the gala, even. Which you would have known if you weren't constantly running away from me."

"Well, you seemed in high demand!" She laughed, somewhat uneasily. Tie stared at her profile for a moment. "If I didn't know better, I'd think you didn't want people to know we came together." He did feel this sense of discomfort every time Laney flitted in and out of his space during the party. She was almost behaving as if she were the hostess, making her rounds and smiling the charming way that she had. It hadn't been bad, because he really made out well, but he could have used her presence more with introductions, especially in the events where the question of his educational background came up. Not often, but often enough to make him feel uncomfortable.

"Did you…" Laney seemed to be considering something, though her eyes were on the road. "Did you get the sense that people were looking at and talking about us when we were together?"

This again? "No, I didn't. But, again, we weren't together that much."

"Well, Ken scowled at us—he's the guy who asked me if I was too good for a brother that day, remember?"

"That prick? I met him. I'd hardly put stock in his opinions."

"Sure, okay, but he was talking to Dante Michaels—the guy on my tenure committee—and they were clearly talking about us." She was stating all this matter-of-factly. "I smiled at Dante—god, my cheeks hurt from smiling so much tonight—but he didn't acknowledge me. He didn't even speak to me all night!" Her voice was wavering a little now. "And a couple of the women, too, were throwing me shade. It was very uncomfortable."

"Like I said, I met Ken. He seemed to sniff at my educational background, but I tried not to pay him any mind."

"You met Ken? You talked to Ken?"

Tie nodded. "I said that." He wondered what party she had been at. Aside from the awkwardness during the very brief conversations about his background, he'd felt rather welcome.

They fell into silence and didn't speak again until she pulled up to her parking spot.

She turned to him as she turned off the ignition. "Do

you mind if we call it an early night? I mean, of course you're always invited to come inside if you like, but I just need a long shower and bed so that I can wake up extra early tomorrow."

He was surprised but tried not to let it show. "That's fine. I'll call you tomorrow, okay?" He gave her a chaste kiss on the lips, knowing anything deeper would have left him with a great deal of sexual tension. He always wanted Laney.

As he pulled out of the parking lot in his own car, he wondered how they managed to see the same majestic sunsets in the same exhilarating way but somehow could not see other events through similar lenses.

Chapter Fourteen

THE SUNDAY BEFORE Thanksgiving, Laney examined her reflection in her standing mirror. Not bad at all. She had spent more time than she cared searching for the right dress to wear to the gala, but she chose well. Anyway, Nette gave her stamp of approval. They had blessedly mended ways the week before.

"Don't you just look like a Barbie? Perfect!" Nette's face beamed in the mirror.

She turned to her friend, smirking. "Again, you test my feminist sensibilities. Well, one thing is for sure. I'm sticking ballet shoes into my clutch because I don't think I'll survive in these stilts all night."

"I'm going to give you a sticker for just having the chutzpah to buy them and put them on. I'm seeing real growth in you, Laney."

Laney rolled her eyes.

"We'd better get going soon, right? Starts at six thirty?"

Laney sucked in a breath. "Yes, that's mingling time, which I could stand to miss. Nette, I really don't want to go tonight. I'm still feeling weird about being in public with Tie, even though this isn't a faculty function. We still haven't addressed my issues head-on. Maybe if I weren't seated at his table…"

Nette put her hands on her hips. "First of all, your concerns are ridiculous—we've already been through that. Secondly, if you really don't want to sit by this hot man who's clearly into you, then you'll probably not have to worry. He'll be up mingling or on the raised platform half the time."

True. But she still wished it weren't so soon after the faculty of color gathering. She still hadn't quite shaken off her prickly qualms about whether they should even continue to see each other. Well, never mind. She'd committed herself to this event, and go she would.

She took a deep breath and looked at Nette, who was stunning in a satin blue dress that made her eyes and hair look sensational. "You're right. At least about your second point. By the way, you really do look incredible tonight. Maybe you'll meet someone. Like you always tell me, you never know."

Nette looked away and Laney immediately regretting bringing up the subject. "Not at all interested. Let's go."

"Okay. We should probably take separate cars because I'm going to have to stay late to help with some of the cleanup."

"No prob." Nette jingled her keys as she walked toward the door.

They simultaneously pulled up to the parking lot, and Nette emerged from her car, smoothing her dress. She waited patiently at first while Laney went through the motions of double-checking the contents of her clutch, reapplying pink cherry lipstick, checking other features in the mirror, taking a tissue out to wipe her nose, checking her nails, which she took the time to get manicured, and—

Thump, thump, thump. Laney turned to see Nette knocking on her window. She read her lips. "Get out!"

Laney sighed and opened the car door. "Okay, okay."

Nette gave Laney a quick squeeze. "You're going to be *fine.*"

The decorations came out nicely. There were festive balloons, and the green was a gorgeous shade one wouldn't expect to see in a balloon. Laney was surprised to see white lilies on each table. Had Tie specifically requested the flowers with her in mind? Silver streamers were draped elegantly. A live band was playing soft instrumentals off to the side. There was even a streamer of dollar bills draped tastefully across the platform at the front of the room. Laney approved of the hall, with its high-hanging lights and generous space. It would easily accommodate the three hundred and fifty or so people they were expecting. She was pleased they went with her suggestion.

Nette immediately recognized people and Laney followed behind. Nette was actually responsible for bringing in several big donors given her connections in the corporate world. As Nette introduced the couple, Laney went through the motions of smiling and shaking hands. Her attention, however, drifted around the room as she wondered about who would be in attendance.

Don't get wigged out, Laney. You belong here as much as anyone. You're not that poor girl from Franklin anymore. Yes.

She knew what she was doing. She'd been to several of these functions with even wealthier people present. And she was a professor, so her quick speaking stint would be easy. Pfft. Everything was tight.

She saw Tie across the room. God, what a sight. Laney was amazed the man could look handsomer than she'd already seen him, but his slim-fitting tux made him look unreal. And the lights were hitting his hair in a way that accentuated his natural golden highlights. She could loosen up and be her usual charming self. She would do it for him.

LANEY WORE A knee-length dress with sparkling, vibrant green sequins and a silver collar. Tie was touched that she thought to coordinate with the theme colors. Emerald-like earrings were radiant in her ears, and her thick hair was neatly pulled up, although a tendril escaped here and there. He was surprised to see strappy silver shoes on her gorgeous feet. She hated heels. She exuded a sense of regality. She owned the room. Tie smiled. She had helped to create this moment. She and Nette were in conversation with a couple of people he didn't know. Well, Nette was in conversation; Laney's head swiveled about.

She spotted him and moved in his direction. Tie noted the turning heads as she walked by. He gave her a kiss on the cheek. Only then did he realize she was a bit nervous. There was a hint of worry in her eyes and her hands were shaking barely.

"What's wrong? Are you okay?" he whispered.

"Yes," she said, looking around, lines creasing her forehead. "I'm just feeling a bit uneasy. I don't know why. I already had a glass of wine at home to calm my nerves, but something isn't feeling quite right."

"Well, everything's good here, partially thanks to you. Everything you were responsible for has been completed, and then some. You look spectacular, by the way."

The worry lines softened a little and she looked into his eyes. "I know tonight will go very well for you, and I'm proud of you for pulling this off. And I plan to have a good time." She smiled and kissed him on the cheek, but he could tell by her shaking hands that she was still nervous.

They headed to their table, where several of his most generous donors were standing or seated. He introduced Laney to each one and offered to get her a drink from the cash bar. As he went to get her a glass of wine he wondered what was bothering her. Lately, they hadn't had much time to discuss anything besides the gala and her work, but he hadn't noticed any anxiety during those times. She wasn't nervous about her brief speaking part, because she was accustomed to speaking in front of people. Well, maybe the wine would help take the edge off.

"WHERE DOES MONEY even come from? How does it get its value? What is credit? What's great about credit? What's not so great about credit? These are the very basic things all kids should know well before heading off on their own." Tie was standing before the microphone on the platform. The gala was in full swing.

Heads bobbed in agreement throughout the room.

"And there's information that could help them get ahead. What is savings? What does it mean to invest? This information is especially crucial for the youth who are least likely to have it—underprivileged kids often from racial or ethnic minority communities. That means, to make such social capital available to youth until it becomes a well-established part of the curriculum, we have to make it financially accessible. That's why you're all here, that's why I'm grateful for your contributions, and I want to let you know that your money is going to a good cause."

There was a steady round of applause.

"It's my pleasure to introduce Dr. Elaine Travers of Sheffield College. She and her colleague plan to implement a program that will increase social capital for incoming students. She'll share a few words about their intentions."

There was light applause as Laney took the microphone from Tie, and he noticed she did not look him in the eye. He walked off to the side, leaving the professor to her own devices.

"Good evening. I'm Laney Travers. As Tie said, my colleague Tracey Harrison and I are attempting to set up a program at Sheffield that would help to provide underprivileged first-year students with the information they need to succeed in college. A big part of the program will focus on financial management. Most of these students come into college with little fiscal knowledge. The type of work Tie is doing will help students in need to be more prepared when they get to college. Tie cares about these students, too, and the communities they come from. You see"—she laughed nervously—"my man doesn't just have jungle fever for women—he has jungle fever for African-American communities… you know, Black people…" She trailed off.

Silence. Subtle sounds of whispering.

Tie froze and suddenly felt nauseated and weak. He quickly regained his composure and hurried over to Laney. Putting his hand on her shoulder, he tried to usher her away from the microphone as tactfully as he could. His stomach and jaw were clenched and his face was growing hotter by the minute. He wanted to shake her and say, "What the hell was that?" But he would have to keep it together.

He walked her down the stairs, fearing she might stumble in her apparent state—though she hadn't stumbled yet and didn't *seem* drunk. In that case, what the hell was she thinking? Where was her head? He left her at the bottom of the steps looking shell-shocked.

He jogged back to the microphone and clasped his hands, a smile plastered on his face. "Thanks again, everyone. Please enjoy the rest of your meal."

There was scattered, light applause across the room, and he hurried off the platform and swept past Laney before anyone could see his face turn red or the sweat beads forming on his forehead.

Chapter Fifteen

LANEY GRABBED HER purse, said a frantic goodbye to her tablemates, eyes averted, and hurried toward the exit. She did not see Tie and certainly was not looking for him.

She heard the clicking of rushed footsteps behind her. That would be Nette. But Laney did not turn around.

Nette grabbed her arm when they reached the lobby, out of the sightline of the grand room. "Laney! Honey, are you okay?"

She didn't look Nette in the eye, but she could tell by her friend's voice that she was concerned. "Not right now. I'll be okay, though. Please go back in. I don't want this to garner any more attention than it already has. Stay here with Tie. It's bad enough I'm running out on him." She turned on her heel and walked to the exit as briskly as the snug evening gown would allow.

"Laney! Why don't we just—"

She didn't hear the rest of Nette's sentence as she hurried toward her car.

She turned on her ignition. What the hell was wrong with her? What had she done? Had her feelings been *that* repressed that they had to come out at the most inopportune moment because of a couple of drinks? No way. No way! But how else to explain her behavior? She imagined herself sitting in front of her former psychotherapist.

So, Elaine, what were you thinking about just prior to the incident? She drew a blank. *What were you feeling just before the incident?* Another blank. This was disturbing. She usually had better self-insight than this.

Before she knew it she was entering the college grounds, and tears started to sting her eyes as they sensed it was finally safe to emerge. Thank goodness the event wouldn't be over for another hour and she wouldn't have to deal with Tie until—

THUMP. Thump.

What the hell? Had she hit something? She wasn't even going the speed limit! She pulled her car over and that was when she immediately saw him in the car headlights. A young man—probably a student. Sprawled beside a mailbox, head down.

Omigod omigod omigod. Laney jumped out of the car.

"Dude!" Two more boys crossed the street to where Lacey was standing. She was frozen momentarily but remembered, numbly, to call 911. Jesus, this couldn't be happening. How had she hit him? He wasn't there, and then somehow he *must* have been. The streetlights in this area were sparse for some reason, and he must have been crossing in the middle of the sidewalk.

One of the boys looked at her accusingly. "What did you do, man?" he demanded. But he knelt by his fallen friend quickly, assisting the other boy in seeing whether he was okay. "He's breathing. I feel his breath," the other boy said.

"Please be careful with his head. He could have a concussion," Laney advised, her own head starting to throb.

"You're giving us advice? Haven't you done enough? Why don't you call an ambulance instead of just standing there!"

"I have called 911!" Laney felt defensive, despite the guilt that was growing exponentially. How had she hit a young man? A college student!

"Can you guys please tell me what happened?" she pleaded. "Did you see anything? I didn't see him cross the street."

"Yeah, he's only a six-foot-two football player. How could you miss him?" came the snarl.

The other boy stood and put his hand on Mr. Snarky's shoulder. "He did just walk into the street—I don't think he looked. To be honest, he's pretty wasted."

"Sean!"

"It's obvious, okay? But then we saw him fly into the air and then land somewhere… I guess here. It's a good thing it's grass. And that you weren't speeding." He scratched his head. "We should have been helping him walk, man."

"He knows how to walk. He can handle his alcohol. If this woman had been looking—"

"Look, blame isn't gonna help Blaine right now, okay?" Sean bent down beside his friend again, moving his hand around beneath him. "I don't see or feel any blood, and he's just wearing a jersey so I think we'd be able to feel it. Don't feel any on his head, either. Maybe just some broken bones? His pulse seems fine. He's just out of it, not waking up. But that could be the booze."

"Good thing season's over." Mr. Snarky glared at Laney.

Laney wasn't sure what to do, having never been in this situation before.

She went to get her purse and fished out her driver's license. Glove compartment for proof of insurance. Did one need that when another vehicle wasn't involved?

The sirens got louder, flashing lights got brighter, and both a squad car and an ambulance arrived simultaneously. The paramedics rushed to the fallen student, performed some quick checks, and got him on the stretcher. His eyes were closed and his head seemed bruised. Laney could already tell that his arm was lying at an unusual angle. She hoped that Sean was right—a few broken bones, at the most.

"Ma'am? Ma'am? We're going to need your statement. You're the driver of this vehicle?"

"Yes," Laney said, dazed. She vaguely noted that a tall, youngish officer was addressing her.

By now, a sizeable crowd had gathered, murmuring things like,

"What happened?"

"Oh, my god, that's Blaine."

"Is he okay?"

"He's alive. They haven't covered him up fully so he'll be okay."

"Is that woman drunk?"

"Wait—is that Dr. Travers?"

"Yes," Laney repeated to the officer, "I'm the one who ran into him, although I was going, like, thirty-four, under the speed limit."

"Fortunately." He made notes on his pad. "Can you tell

me what happened?"

Laney recounted the little that she witnessed, adding the part where his friends had come over to inspect the body, and what she overheard about his drinking.

"Well, he was definitely jaywalking, and the lighting is poor around here. I'm surprised the college hasn't addressed this." He had soft brown eyes, and Laney felt a little more at ease. "Look, it was an accident. No one is saying you're at fault, although we do have to get all the witness statements. My partner is talking to the boys now."

"Of course."

"License and registration?" Oh, registration. Laney went back to the glove compartment. The beam from the officer's flashlight followed her into the car. "Yes, it's in here, somewhere…"

"Ma'am?"

"Yes?"

"Have you been drinking tonight?"

"No. I mean yes, but not like them." She nodded toward Blaine and his friends.

The officer glanced at her dress. "Look, it doesn't matter the type of drink or the venue, alcohol is alcohol." He moved aside. "Can you please step back fully out of the vehicle?"

Laney did as she was told. It felt like her heart was going to drive through her chest.

"I'm going to need to run a Breathalyzer on you. This is standard procedure when there's drinking involved in a collision."

The murmuring got louder as the crowd grew. Laney had

never had a Breathalyzer test in her life, and now she was expected to do it in front of students? When was she going to wake up from this humiliating nightmare? She took a deep, shaky breath.

"Okay. Thanks for cooperating. BAC point oh-five."

Her eyebrows raised and her heart thumped.

"It's okay. You get an OVI over point oh-eight. You're clear."

Well, she had done one thing right this evening—avoided drunkenness. Although god knew everyone likely thought she was intoxicated.

"Yeah, can you please announce that a little more loudly, since you performed a Breathalyzer in front of all my students?" Laney's heart was still racing.

The cop looked at her with surprise for a moment. "Hey, Ellis," he called over to his partner. "Driver's BAC in the clear."

The murmurs in the crowd grew louder, and Laney's cheeks were hot despite the late November nip.

"Well, that's certainly not the story on this end," Ellis responded. "I can tell you without a Breathalyzer."

The cop turned back to her. "Loud enough to your liking?"

Laney nodded. "Thank you," she whispered.

"If you're willing, I need you to come down to the station with me to answer some further questions."

"The station? Why? I told you everything."

"We'd like to corroborate your story. The boys'll be going into the station, too. Besides, I'd think you'd want to get out of this crowd."

That was true. But in a squad car? "Am I under arrest?"

"No, ma'am, but it would help to complete this investigation."

Investigation. How had Laney ended up in this mess?

"Okay, whatever helps. I just leave my car here?"

"For now, if you don't mind."

She switched off her ignition, ignoring the churning in her stomach, the internal cacophony. "Okay, ready when you are. Just, for god's sake, don't cuff me."

Chapter Sixteen

"LANEY."

She came down the hall at the police station, looking as frightened and as vulnerable as he'd ever seen her. She would still a be a beautiful sight to anyone who passed, but Tie saw the unshed tears in her eyes and noted her hair was no longer in a neat twist. Seeing that she was physically unharmed, though, caused him to let out a long breath that he had not realized he'd been holding onto. He held his arms out, and she tentatively went to him. As he embraced her, he noticed that she pulled into herself, almost as if protecting herself from him. He kissed her on top of the head. "It's okay, sweetie. It's over now. We'll deal with all the other stuff later."

She shuddered against him, and she suddenly looked up. "What about the student? Any word on him? How'd you even know about any of this?"

Tie patted her on the back. "Yes, I talked to Nenette again while waiting for you. He'll make a full recovery, eventually. Ironically, the mailbox that he was slammed into broke his fall and probably saved his head, although he does have several broken bones. And," he added, although this probably wouldn't sound like good news to the person who was behind the wheel, "um… likely a concussion from the impact of the fall. He's lucid, though! I should say, all of this comes via Nenette, so take it with a grain of salt."

Laney put her head onto his chest and was quiet for a few moments.

"If anyone has the scoop this early in the game," she said into his chest, "it would be Nette. I do have several missed calls from her. She's glued to social media." She smiled briefly, sadly. "That's why I was so reticent to tell her about us in the beginning. It could have been broadcasted on Twitter within seconds."

She suddenly pushed him away and shook her head. "I don't deserve you. Look what I've made of this evening! Look at what I've dragged you into. You're picking me up from a police station, for goodness' sake!"

"Shhhh." He put a finger to her lips and then took her by the hand. "We'll talk about everything at home, okay? I do have a lot of questions, but first I wanted to make sure that you were okay. At least, physically," he added.

Laney seemed to notice an officer watching them out of the corner of his eye, because she didn't put up any further resistance and let Tie lead her out the door. They drove to her house in silence. For the umpteenth time that night, he wondered what was going on in her complex mind. His stomach clenched as he recalled her stage performance, but he immediately suppressed it, wanting to focus on getting her settled at home. He sighed, reached over, and placed his hand atop hers, then drew it to his lips for a kiss. That was the only communication he attempted, giving them both time to collect their thoughts.

"I guess I should have had you drop me off at my car, which is parked on a street near here," Laney surprised him by finally saying as they pulled up in front of her house.

"Oh. We can attend to that once you've gotten a bit of rest."

Her head was down as she seemed to be avoiding any possible eye contact with her neighbors. With her living so near campus, many of them had already likely heard about the accident and might even know that a Sheffield professor and student were involved, if not what configuration and names. He put an arm around her waist. He wished he could rewind the clock to early evening. Dash whatever possessed her to say what she'd said at the gala, and none of this ever would have happened.

If Nette's sources were correct, Laney hadn't gotten an OVI. Though mostly relieved for her, he had mixed feelings. Again, his stomach clenched as clearer visions of the charity event came into focus. If she hadn't been intoxicated, then, truly, what the hell was going on? She could not, would not, sabotage him. But her stunt did not look good to donors and potential supporters. She had left a mess under the rug for him to deal with.

She paused at the door. Her eyebrows shot up as she turned toward Tie.

He nodded.

Once inside he removed his shoes and joined Laney, who had made a beeline for the kitchen.

Tie thought he could make them some tea or, from the

looks of her, some coffee. He was surprised when she came out of the fridge with a bottle of sauvignon blanc in her hand. She started toward the cabinet, asking over her shoulder, "Do you want a glass?"

"Laney." His voice came out much harsher than he'd intended, and he saw her jump.

She spun around. "What, what's wrong?" Tie looked pointedly at the bottle of wine and then back at her wide eyes. Her eyes trailed his.

"Oh, my god." She put the back of her hand up to her forehead then down onto her hip. "I didn't even think. This might be what got me into this mess, right? But I had such a bad night... the first thing... need a drink. I mean it's just wine but—" She looked at him. She started to put the wine back in the fridge, changed her mind and poured it down the sink. Tapping her fingers on the counter, she asked, "Coffee sound okay?"

He nodded. "It sounds perfect, really."

They were silent as the coffee brewed. Then she talked him into sitting down, letting him know that she was just feeling too antsy to sit at the moment.

When she placed a steaming mug before each of them, he cleared his throat. She glanced at him expectantly.

"You're lucky you didn't get an OVI."

"I knew I wasn't drunk. I wasn't even tipsy. I really didn't have to go down to the station. I was just helping them out."

Well, that settled it. She had been sober. He clasped his fingers together, elbows on the table, took a breath, and looked directly at her. He thought she shivered. He didn't doubt that anger was beginning to be reflected in his eyes, as he felt the hotness in his chest. "Laney. What the hell happened? At the gala. You know what I mean."

Her mouth opened and closed a couple of times. "Of course, I know what you mean. But I don't know what got into me. I guess I was just feeling certain things that I hadn't articulated." Her voice seemed dry.

He took a couple of slow breaths, trying to slow his heart rate. "Do you need some water?"

"I'm good."

Still dry.

"Laney, why would tonight, in front of everyone I know, be the right time to articulate feelings you hadn't articulated before?" His voice had an edge, but he couldn't keep his tone much more even than it was at present.

She looked at him like he had slapped her. "I don't know! You can't believe that I did that on purpose!"

He threw his hands up. The control in his voice disappeared as he bellowed, "I don't know what to believe!"

She sat back and began wiping her eyes with the back of her hand.

As angry as he was, his heart was breaking for her. He looked away from her face so he could continue. "Did I do something to you? Are you angry with me for something?"

She was silent for a full minute or two.

"Tie. Let's face it. You're a White man and I'm a Black woman. There's a world of difference between us."

His head jerked up. What? Where did that come from,

suddenly? "There would be a world of difference between me and many other women I could be with. So? How has it gotten in the way? Have I done something wrong?"

"No, no, nothing like that." She met his stare. "I just wonder if it's always going to be in our way."

His chest tightened. "I'm sorry, I *still* have no fucking clue what you're talking about. Can you enlighten me, Professor? What is it I'm too stupid to understand? In what way is my background hindering the progress of our relationship?"

Her eyebrows drew together and the corners of her mouth turned down. "I never called you stupid. So don't go there. I just... like you don't get that other Black people, especially the men, give us dismissive looks when we're out together. You don't get that threat of discomfort."

He rolled his eyes. "Discomfort for whom?"

She looked at him desperately. "Well, me for one. And others who aren't big on Black-White relationships, probably... please, Tie, try to understand from my perspective. I'm not saying things are completely hopeless, because I just don't really know. I guess I just need some time to figure things out. I don't know. Please understand me."

He stood up and sighed, his hands akimbo. "No, I'm not going to make this easy for you, Laney. My heart is in jeopardy here, and you still haven't given me a goddamn logical reason for why you'd sabotage me in front of everyone. This *must* be about something else. Has my lack of education finally become too much for you to bear? Is that why you don't want me around your colleagues?" He began to feel light-headed.

"God, no! Why would you think that? Nothing like that. That's why this is so hard. But I want to do things right. I'm trying to be open with you. You told me I could tell you anything."

"No, no... you don't get to use that against me. You don't get to just tell me about myself in this relationship. And I don't feel transparency here, because none of this makes any goddamn sense. We've been in public, and it's been wonderful. For god's sake, that faculty of color gathering was a great experience. I still wonder if we were at the same function, Laney. I don't know why you're manufacturing excuses to break us apart. And I certainly don't get why you'd fuck me by doing this in public." His teeth were clenched.

Laney's tears continued to stream and he had to look away from her again. "It wasn't intentional. And I'm not even sure that the two are related. I don't *want* to break us up! I just want to be in this relationship with a clear head, and I haven't been able to have a really clear head since I met you. I try to think, but then something takes over and pulls me into this... this... magical world that we've created for ourselves, and my thoughts get scrambled until I'm alone again."

Tie sighed. He was relieved that she wasn't gearing toward a breakup. "Our relationship is different, Laney. It *is* magical. It's intense. It's unlike anything I've ever experienced. And if that's mind-blowing and defies intellectual analysis, I fail to see how it's a bad thing."

Laney covered her face with her hands and started sobbing.

He couldn't stand seeing her this way, as angry as he was. He unclenched his fists; his fingernails had been digging into his palms. He walked around to her and took her into his arms. He smoothed her hair and kissed the top of her head. She still seemed to pull into herself. He rocked her gently from side to side. Her sobs eventually subsided. He didn't know what to do or say next. She was not going to give him any reasonable explanation for why she embarrassed him in front of his colleagues, friends, and associates. Not tonight, anyway. He would just have to focus on damage control. It seemed as though their relationship needed it as much as his reputation.

"Baby, why are you doing this to yourself? To us?"

Her tears let up and she sniffled, looking up at him. "I just need you to understand. And the fact that you don't understand just reinforces my concerns."

"You've concluded that I don't understand, Professor, but I think I do understand how your mind is working, churning out problems that don't exist. I just don't *agree*. And if you have the hubris to assume that your perspective is the correct perspective, then there are indeed some fundamental issues at hand." He dropped his arms from her back and took a step back. He ran his fingers through his hair. "I don't know. Maybe you're right. You're the one with the PhD, right? Doing something meaningful with your life," he spat out. "Treat me like the idiot I am and break this crap down into something an idiot can understand and *believe*."

His fists were clenched again.

This emotional roller coaster was becoming too much to stand.

"Tie, don't be like that! It's not just my perspective! Dissertation theses and books are out there on the subject of this, specifically, White men and Black women couples reenacting an oppressive relationship based in slavery. I'm sure you can get that."

He threw his hands up. "My god, Laney. Really? Yes, I do know basic history, idiot or not. But I don't care about the academics of the matter. I only care about us!" His voice boomed.

"It's not just academic." She blinked slowly and sighed. "I'm becoming a liability to you, too. Look what happened tonight. I cannot believe this night!" She shook her head as her eyes widened.

He stared at her. She thought of him as a *liability*? Seriously? To what? And now she was calling herself a liability. Well… she didn't exactly promote his cause tonight.

"If you think of me as a liability, Laney—"

"Liability wasn't a good word. At least not for you. But you saw how I was tonight in front of all your people."

"I hardly think that's typical of you. I have no idea what tonight's thing was about, but I have confidence that you wouldn't do it again."

She sniffled. "But it's already been done."

He was silent. She certainly had a point there.

She seemed to be pleading with her eyes. He was unaccustomed to seeing her look helpless.

He looked down. "Is this bullshit going to end if you get—when you get—tenure? Will you then feel proven enough as an academic that you can make decisions based upon how you feel, not just how you think—or how you *think* you should think? Shall I call you up after your tenure decision?" He paused. "If I'm still available."

"Wait—I never said—"

"Never said what, Laney? Never said we're going to break up? You're practically talking me into running in the other direction!"

Laney tried one last appeal. "I just wanted you to understand where all this discomfort is coming from. Too many people would see me—I'm sure do see me—as being a traitor to Black men."

"Wh—you a traitor to Black men? Like whom? Like your father?"

Anger flared in her face. This last statement went too far. But he was desperate.

She screamed. Just screamed. And cried. And stared at him through a curtain of tears.

He looked down again.

"I just knew this was such a bad idea, to try to be fully honest with you!"

She ran up the stairs, and her bedroom door slammed.

He did not try to stop her.

THE TOILET RULE. They'd never seen each other at their

angriest until now—and they didn't endure it. Enduring it might have been the only lifeline for leaving behind the despair and saving their relationship.

He'd made her feel like a princess. She'd lost her prince.

Chapter Seventeen

L ANEY TRIED TO suck her vanilla milkshake through a straw. She and Tracey had found a table away from the windows, per Laney's suggestion. If she wouldn't have looked ridiculous with huge black sunglasses on, she would have found some to wear. Instead, she took another look and saw that there were few people around, most going through the drive-thru, and those eating in were mostly tired-looking mothers and their children.

Despite Laney's intentions, she had panicked at the last minute and avoided campus, doing work in her home office. She just wasn't ready to face it. Tie had been enough.

"Thanks for meeting me here, Trace. I know it's not an ideal lunch spot, but it's one place I know we're unlikely to run into our snobby colleagues. The occasional student, maybe, but they usually eat on campus."

"This is true." Tracey took her salad and water from her tray and placed the tray atop a nearby waste can. Laney felt a bit piggish with her double Quarter Pounder, fries, and milkshake, but she figured since she was at the fast-food giant on one of the rare occasions she might as well go all out. She was famished, mysteriously. Usually when depressed or anxious—and she was both—she couldn't eat.

"So… what have you heard?"

Tracey, who was wearing a white silk blouse, squeezed her salad dressing packet very gently before picking up a fork and stabbing iceberg lettuce. "Well, you know I'm like a snail on social media, so I didn't hear anything 'til this morning."

"I really have to introduce you to Nenette. That way you won't even need any of your accounts. Just a cell phone for her texts and calls."

"Yeah, you keep saying that. I'm starting to think she's your imaginary friend. Anyway, I do have a couple of student friends on Facebook—just my research students—and I saw a few pictures and some comments from last night." She paused and gave Laney a cautionary look. "You sure you wanna go there?"

Laney sighed and looked toward the window. "It's okay; I'm prepared for the worst. Nette said Instagram was blowing up last night."

"Well"—Tracey tucked some paper napkins into her collar, looking ridiculous but practical—"students like you, so I don't think you have to worry about anyone really bad-mouthing you. The comments sections seemed to reflect students' understanding that you weren't drunk and didn't get an OVI." She paused.

"Yes, they're right," Laney confirmed.

"Some are speculating on whether you'd beat them at drinking games, what you're like when you're drunk… nonsense like that."

Her face warmed. This wouldn't go away anytime soon.

"Anybody faulting me for the accident?"

"I couldn't tell, but maybe a few guys on the football team. You know, Blaine is one of our players."

Laney nodded. "Yes, I dealt with one of his cronies last night." She removed the pickles from her burger, swearing that she distinctly asked for them to be left off. "What about our colleagues? That's not as likely to come through Facebook or Insta, but maybe Twitter."

"Well, I don't have a Twitter account, but I do have Gina Takis in my department, as you know. So she was pretty much sticking her head in everyone's door this morning saying, 'Did you hear…' I think the conversations were pretty short. Nobody gives a damn what Gina has to say unless she's found out something related to the faculty as a whole. I think most folks had questions about whether the student was okay and whether you'd been under the influence."

Laney sighed. "Beyond that?"

"I couldn't really tell. Like I said, the conversations seemed pretty short. But most of us probably considered it non-news and have better things to do this close to finals. I will say that Keith came by when Gina wasn't around and asked me whether I thought you'd be sanctioned by administration."

Keith, a biologist, was another of Laney's friends, although they rarely got together.

She sighed. "I already have a meeting with Sharon, set for tomorrow. That quickly." She was referring to the email message she had earlier received from the provost, requesting a meeting. It was at that point, sitting in her car, that Laney decided that she wasn't yet ready to face campus.

Tracey grimaced. "Ouch. But really, what can they do? You didn't break a law! Really none of their business." She shook her head no when Laney offered her fries.

"Well, you seem to keep forgetting that we're not yet tenured. We're awash in politics."

"But you're an academic sweetheart. You're in good with the administration. It would be different if you were found doing shots with a freshman."

"If only everyone would use that image as a point of reference," Laney responded grimly.

"Listen, it's not like anyone expects us to be teetotalers. Look how much our colleagues put down during sherry hours. That's the only reason people go to faculty functions and the Christmas party—which I hope you'll attend with me. Plus, I bet at least a quarter of the faculty have a flask in their drawer or else alcohol hidden somewhere in the office. Why not? We practically live there."

"Do you?" She watched Tracey closely.

Tracey was a few shades darker than Laney, but Laney could tell that her colleague's face was warming. "Well, no. You know I'm not much of a drinker. But I don't judge those who are."

"Well, I guess I have to go to campus tomorrow anyway. Two classes. It's kind of good I'm being forced to get it out of the way."

"Pfft." Tracey waved her hand. "All your students are going to care about is their final grade. From day one that's been their concern. What's new? You could be a mass murderer, but as long as you're their professor, their grade would be their top concern."

"You're right. Cheers!" Laney said, holding up her now squishable milkshake.

Tracey brought her bottle of water up to meet the milkshake. "Cheers. To what, by the way?"

"To grade-grubbing students, faculty functions, academic amnesia, and the short news cycle of social media."

"Oh, okay." Tracey looked confused.

THAT EVENING, LANEY walked down the hospital hallway, having been directed to Blaine's room. Visiting hours were nearly over; she was late because she had procrastinated the visit. She was scared. Of what she'd find in the hospital bed, of his family, of what this all meant. She peeked into the room. It was just Blaine, no parents or other visitors. She breathed a sigh of relief. At first, he seemed to be sleeping but then she noticed his eyes were only half-closed.

They popped open fully when he noticed her. "Hey, Dr. Travers, right?"

Laney nodded and neared the bed. He had flowers and balloons adorning every spare surface in the room.

"Hi, Blaine. I'm sorry this had to be how we met."

"Yeah. I would shake your hand, but…"

Laney glanced at the cast on his left arm and the cast around his right wrist. The poor guy was going to struggle for a while.

A lump grew in her throat. "I'm so sorry about this, Blaine. If I could take your injuries upon myself…"

"Hey, hey! No, man. I know this was an accident. They told me you weren't even going the speed limit. I was wasted; I own that much." His glazed eyes stayed on her. Well, the medication wasn't doing him any harm.

"Well, I should let you get some rest."

"Sit," Blaine ordered. "Talking takes my mind off all this, and this is the first time I've been alone all day."

Laney did as she was told.

"So," he began. "Were you coming from a party? They said you were blinging."

Laney gave him a weak smile. She certainly didn't want to recall the events of that evening, but she felt obligated to Blaine. "Well, yes. It was a gala…"

When visiting hours ended thirty minutes later, Laney walked back down the hallway toward the exit. One hospital visit per a semester was her maximum capacity.

Chapter Eighteen

T HE PROVOST TOOK a deep breath after closing the door and sitting down. "Laney... wow, this is difficult." Pause. "Laney, you know I'm not the one who does the official decision making when it comes to hires and... contract terminations."

Laney's stomach tightened.

"But part of my job is to discuss those contracts with our faculty. I've gotten to know you over these past five years, and it has been a privilege to know you and your work. I have a lot of respect for you. But"—she looked at her knees, brushing invisible lint from her impeccable gray trousers—"we have certain key values to uphold as members of the college community. And I think you know that you've recently skirted at least one of those values."

Laney kept her eyes focused on Sharon, trying to look undaunted. But she hoped she wouldn't have to speak soon, as her mouth was bone-dry. Which value, exactly, had she infracted?

The provost met her eyes. "You know there is a character clause in the faculty handbook, just as there is in the student and staff handbooks. This is an essential element of living in a spiritual community. Now, we don't think it's ethical to make you wait until your tenure decision to find out that your contract has been terminated. But we also cannot with any certainty conclude that your actions warrant termination at this time. You certainly haven't broken any public laws." She waited, searching Laney's eyes to see if her words had sunken in.

"So," she continued uncertainly, "I want to let you know that you will be receiving an official communication from the president's office, letting you know that you are being placed on probationary status and outlining the terms of this status for next semester."

Probationary status? Laney had never even heard of such, at least not for faculty, at any academic institution. Was this even in the faculty handbook? She caught her breath—this was a relatively *good* thing, considering the worst-case scenario.

"If you successfully pass probation at semester end, then you will return to your tenure track status."

Laney still managed to keep her eyes focused on Sharon's despite her heart pounding in her throat and her head feeling very, very light. If she hadn't envisioned the worst-case scenario, she likely would have passed out from shock.

Sharon leaned forward. "I know this whole situation is awkward, Elaine, and no one could blame you if you didn't want to renew your contract for next year even after a successful probationary period. But I want you to know that I'm more than happy to write a letter of recommendation on your behalf if that should be the case, because I think I know you and your work well. I don't think this incident is a reflection of who you are as a person." She straightened again. "We know that, ultimately, it was an accident. And I know that a number of your colleagues would also be willing to testify to your strengths, for wherever you decide to go from here. Off the record, we really value your presence and would be distressed to see you go. Consider me a friend. Consult with me about anything, and that should certainly be the case if you leave. You wouldn't be 'under' me any longer, after all." She shrugged.

Laney believed her. But this probation status still sounded a bit... conjured? Which could get the college into legal trouble if it didn't go her way. And Sharon's "off the record" statement seemed to assure that Laney would be allowed to stay on unless she really bungled something up. Maybe this "probation" was just a formality, a message to send to the college community but had no real bearing on anything official. At least, that was the best she could hope for.

But what if the administration knew more of her background? She was pretty sure that being a stripper was a breach of any character clause. If this fact was going to constitute more "bungling," she wanted to have the cards laid out sooner than later. But they couldn't know about her background. No one did. She'd leave it alone.

Silence ensued. Laney swallowed, to the extent that her dry throat and pounding heart allowed, and tried to steady herself. "Thanks, Sharon. I know this is hard for you. I don't take it personally. I know you're only doing your job." She was amazed at how smooth her voice sounded, given how tense she was. "Um, I'll think about your offer of that recommendation letter if things should come to that. Look, I'll have my work cut out for me next semester—although it's hard to wrap my mind around it considering we're buried by the culmination of the current semester. But at the moment, I have to say I'm most consumed with guilt about what happened. It was fortunate that the student came out mendable."

"You've said your apologies, I'm sure. It was an accident, not truly your fault, and you need to put it behind you. The fact that it was a student, well, that complicated things, didn't it? And the fact that you had indeed been drinking, well, we know that was the rusty nail. But that particular nail is yours to deal with, and you really don't owe anyone an explanation. My suggestion is to move on. Be open to the student's family should they reach out to you further, but otherwise move on. You have work to do." She winked.

It sure feels like my fault. Had I not been distracted... But she swept the thought aside before she lost the nerve to continue. "Thank you, Sharon. You don't know how much anyone's support means to me right now—and especially coming from top brass at Sheffield."

"Pshaw. Top brass." Sharon waved her hand good-naturedly. "So, do you have any questions for me?"

"Not at the moment." She did not acknowledge the big question of where this "probation" status suddenly came from. "I just have a lot of thinking and soul searching to do."

"Indeed. Well then." The provost rose to her feet and went toward the door. "We'll meet again, at least once more, next semester?"

Laney nodded. She'd kept it together for this long, but she was through with talking.

Sharon opened the door. "Bye, then."

Laney smiled goodbye and turned into the hallway, avoiding anyone's eyes as she walked past.

Chapter Nineteen

A S A PROGRESSIVE thinker, Tie nearly growled at anyone who accused another of "playing a card," be it race, religion, sexuality, gender, or whatever. Social justice wasn't a game, although it indeed had to be won, or attained. Still, he didn't want to accept that their fight, and likely the end of their relationship, had come down to race. As simple as that. And not their problem with race, but others'. Or, at least as she construed it. What the fuck? The growth of his relationship with Laney, that was larger than life itself, more expansive than the universe, and now it was preempted due to racial politics? He couldn't stand it. Had he known this would be an issue, he wouldn't have even considered dating a Black woman more than casually, no matter how breathtaking she was in beauty and intelligence.

He slammed his fist on the marble countertop and grimaced. As he rubbed his fist, he considered how great he and Laney seemed. How awesome they could be together. He did not consider himself vain, but seeing their reflection in the mirror at the entrance to a WYQT function had stunned him. How could such an attractive, complementary couple not be right for each other? How could someone who sounded, tasted, smelled, and *felt* so perfect not be his? His soul felt at home with her. Breaking up didn't make sense. Their presence made other people happy and comfortable— aside from those who, according to Laney, gave them dirty looks when he wasn't watching. But Laney was bright and insightful. She couldn't be imagining such things, and her argument had to have some sense.

Shit! For once he wished he hosted another radio program, one in which he could cover social issues of interest. He wished he had studied more in the other social sciences. Maybe then he'd be better adept at arguing her on this issue. Not for the first time, he regretted dropping out of college. Years of self-teaching apparently didn't compensate for formal education.

He stood on his balcony and looked at the lighted fountain in the pond. This was not okay. This was not meant to be a real thing, this breakup. He and Laney were both ambitious despite the odds. Neither of them would be where they were today if otherwise was the case. They had to be able to work this out together.

Unless…

Was this whole thing a ruse, just to end the relationship? Maybe it wasn't that Tie wasn't Black enough, but rather he simply wasn't good enough. He had no PhD, and though he could hold his own in conversation with the smartest minds in the world, it didn't change the fact that he simply wasn't one of them. Had her colleagues said something to her to make her second-guess his worth? He bit his lip. He missed her painfully, but if she really didn't want him, why should he subject himself to more rejection?

He heard his father's voice.

"A B? You're bringing home a B? This is unacceptable, Tie. It's just AP calculus, for chrissakes. What are you going to do when you get to college? Are we going to have to send you to a state school?"

"Look, you chose me, remember? You knew I wouldn't have your genes! You knew I wouldn't be perfect like Father!"

"And you should be grateful that we chose you, dammit! There aren't many who would take on a five-year-old boy, no matter how gorgeous your mother says you were. The only reason you caught my *eye was because you were gifted. So this is about your potential, not my genes!"*

He knew that he was adopted, but at five? This was the first he'd heard of that. He'd always assumed that he'd been adopted at birth.

Did someone give him up when he was five? Or was he in the orphanage all that time? Either way, he must have been a mess.

He wasn't about to ask his father… he was likely to find out something he really didn't want to know, and from someone who didn't give a damn.

"There are other gifted kids, you know, and not everyone gets to be valedictorian. I have other things going on, and I'm sorry I can't achieve perfect grades every term. It's not for lack of trying, and you know that."

"I don't care about other kids. You're the one I adopted."

"Well, I'm sorry I didn't come with a damn refund policy!"

"Don't you curse at me, boy."

"Fuck it!"

He got no sleep that night, wrestling with his conflicting

emotions and missing Laney's soft skin. ·

THEY HAD EXCEEDED their fundraising goal by approximately $23,000. Tie couldn't be happier. The only cloud in the program development sky was the prospect of losing any of those pledged funds or future funds. Grants would always be an option, pretty much regardless of his local reputation, but individuals were another matter.

In the middle of reviewing the sketch of his show, Tie received a phone call. It was from the CFO of a local Black-owned real estate business.

"Hi, Ron!"

"Hi, Tie. Um, listen. Mike and I wanted to follow up with you about the gala."

Tie's stomach started to knot. "Sure. Thanks again for your generous contribution. It will help us do a world of good."

"Yes, well, we hope so. Because as much as we think this program could benefit youth, we want them to be empowered, not patronized. Yes, they're children, but we want them to start thinking like adults and thinking for themselves."

"I couldn't agree more, Ron."

"You know, the teach-a-man-to-fish philosophy, rather than the White knight riding in with sacks of fish to throw at the hapless crowd."

Tie was silenced. He pictured Ron's intense brownish-black eyes on the other end.

"Or, even worse, exploiting Black youth to win diversity points toward an ulterior goal."

Wow. Just, wow. Tie had no doubt where these concerns were coming from.

"That would be egregious, Ron, and I can assure you that neither of those are my intentions. I'm really invested in leveling the playing field when it comes to financial literacy. My gir—Dr. Travers misspoke at the function and has since apologized profusely." Not quite the truth about Laney, but she was contrite in her heart.

Ron cleared his throat. "That's good to hear. But you have to wonder. I mean, statements like that don't just come out of the blue. Especially from an esteemed individual."

"Yes, well, I can't explain—she was bewildered herself about having said such remarks, so… I can only assure you that they had no basis in reality."

There was a pause on the other end. "Okay, Tie. Thanks for taking time out."

"And thank you so much again for your generous gift."

He had no doubt that Ron and Mike would delegate someone to do a bit of behind-the-scenes research on Tie. Past interviews, leads on Google, whatever. Thank goodness they wouldn't find anything incriminating.

Tie wished that were the only such conversation he had in the weeks following the gala, but this was not the case.

ROUTINE AND OCCUPATION were the only things keeping

Tie sane. He tried not to think beyond his routine. Tried harder not to feel.

Tie decided to video chat with his sister. He was used to visiting her frequently when he was in Chicago, and that was something he missed doing. Now, he frequently chatted with her.

"Meghan! Hi!"

"Hi, Tie!"

"How are you, my favorite big sis?"

"I am happy. Donald is happy," she said, referring to her new husband.

"That's what I want to hear. You know I miss you, right?"

Meghan rolled her eyes, giggling. "Yes, yes. You tell me almost every day. I miss you too."

"But you have Donald there, and I'm glad he makes you happy."

"We had a picnic yesterday. We stayed inside because it's too cold. But it was fun!"

"That sounds awesome."

"Are you happy, Tie?"

The question caught Tie off guard, although his sister was sweet and sensitive, always asking whether he was happy. He could usually say yes, or talk his way around it, but when things were really a mess, as they were at present, he was bumped into the uncomfortable position of having to present things in a different light.

"Well, I'm okay, honey bear." He really needed to stop calling her that, especially now that she was married. And she was, after all, his older sister, and the nickname sounded too cute, condescending. "Just, when you move, there's a lot of new stuff to get used to. A lot of things happen that can make you kind of forget who you are."

Meghan giggled. "If you forget, you call me and I will say your name is Tie Stevens and you have a sister named Meghan."

He clasped his hands. "You know what? That would actually help a lot. You can be my rock."

Meghan tilted her head.

"Okay, lovely. I'm glad to hear you're well. I'll chat with you again soon."

"Bye, Tie. Don't forget who you are."

Tie sat thinking about her simple words. Sometimes his sister, despite her Down syndrome, imparted the most helpful wisdom. She would have some simple humanity-based advice for Laney regarding this inane race problem. He really missed Meghan. She really was his rock. Donald, who also had intellectual disabilities, seemed like a funny, friendly young man, and one of the only reasons Tie had left Chicago was knowing enough about him.

No, he couldn't burden her with his problems, not that she would immediately understand them, anyway. Hell, he barely understood them himself.

TIE WAS IN the middle of crunches at the gym when he decided he would answer his cell. Usually, workout time was sacred time, whether he fit it in during his usual morning routine, at lunchtime, or the occasional evening. But he recognized the ringtone—"Freebird"—as his buddy Craig, whom he didn't get to speak to as much as he would have liked, even back in Chicago. He was a fraternity brother from college.

"Hey, man!" Tie answered, panting.

"Working out or slightly boring sex?"

Tie guffawed. "You know me well enough—which could I be doing at seven in the morning?"

"Morning sex is rarely boring, so I'm gonna say working out."

"Told you you know me, man."

"How's Columbus, and when are you going to wake up and realize that you're in the wrong city, bro?"

Tie chuckled. "Not anytime soon, guy."

"I don't get it. At all. You loved Chicago. Meg's here. Hell—I'm here... there are no major sports teams out there..."

Tie took a long drink from his water bottle. "Well, I have to admit, I miss being taken along for some of your crazy rides." Tie smiled. "You played hard, like a baller."

"I know you don't make that much less than me. You're just too practical, with your conservative investments and savings accounts."

"Total geek, I know."

"But, really, I'm sure I can come up with an excuse to go to Columbus."

"You need an excuse to see me now?"

"You know what I mean. A billable reason."

Tie wiped the sweat from his brow. "I told you about the nonprofit camp I want to develop here. Excellent opportunity for consulting. Even better, excellent opportunity for donating. I forgot to hit you up."

"You know I'd never bill you, bro. As for the donation, of course. If you haven't reached some of our connections here in Chicago, I can reach out to them as well. They're always looking to sponsor something. That wouldn't mean you're off the hook for not coming to your senses and making a hairpin turn for Chicago. I can't enable craziness. Wait a minute. Stevens, don't tell me. Is it a woman?"

Tie sipped on his water. Craig knew him way too damn much. It was why he bothered striking up a friendship with a guy who initially seemed obnoxious.

"You think being silent is gonna make me forget the question?"

"Guy, do you really think I would make a decision like moving from Chicago, along with my entire show, based upon a woman? I was only here for a few days in August."

Now Craig was silent. "Not typically, but you're a romantic at heart—don't even try to deny it. I know you. I wouldn't have bet on it, but Tie Stevens might have finally found a girl to make him really take notice. Well, I made you wear the monkey suit for my wedding, so just say the word, dude."

"Don't take it there."

"Oh, so there is an 'it,' though. What's she like?"

Tie was feeling strangely protective and possessive suddenly. He and Craig usually talked about women like the closest of brothers. "She's just... Laney. Beautiful."

"Obviously."

"Smart."

"Again, obviously."

Tie shrugged, not wanting to try articulating why he was especially drawn to Laney. More than anyone else had ever come close to doing, she made him feel at his best, like he was good enough. At least, usually. The breakup really made him question everything again. And he had no desire to put his painful emotions on display this morning, even with Craig.

"Okay." Craig sighed. "I'll fill in some of the other blanks for you, since you're suddenly into phone charades. She's sexy as hell and you have amazing sex. Yup. Sometimes that's all there is to it, assuming she's not a bitch."

Tie cringed. "Okay, man, you got it. Look, you'll just have to come through Columbus to see for yourself."

"Yeah, we'll see. Hey, I remember you assured me they have beer in Ohio, but you could only name one original. So are you gonna be able to have the best indigenous beers for me to try when I visit, or what? Besides that—what was it? Hungry Hippo?"

"Thirsty Dog. And as a matter of fact you might be surprised. There's a CBC Creeper with your name all over it. Columbus Brewing Company." Tie paused. "So, have you heard from Mike?"

"Yeah, I think he called a couple of weeks ago, now that you mention it. Wanted to grab lunch or something." Tie could tell that Craig was trying to sound as casual as possible.

Tie remained silent. He hadn't heard from his father in months. Since his birthday in March. At that time, his mother had called, then argued with his old man to get him on the phone.

"But I haven't had the time to take him up on lunch. And really, you know I don't feel comfortable with his pretending I'm his… younger self or something. I never asked for that," Craig uncomfortably added.

"I know you didn't. But take it as a compliment. I told you it means he thinks you've amounted to something noble in his eyes."

Craig snorted. "The only person on earth who could view me that way."

"I mean, you got a PhD. And do you still teach evening classes, in addition to the consulting?"

"Yeah."

He could tell Craig was feeling uneasy. Tie didn't mean to make his friend uncomfortable, and it wasn't like Tie needed further evidence that his father thought his own son wasn't worth his time.

"And you don't teach for the money, that's for sure. That's pretty noble."

"Anyway…" Craig sighed. "I don't know if I'm gonna have time to see him any time soon."

They were both silent for a while.

"How's Vanessa?" Craig's wife was a safe topic.

"Vanessa's pregnant, bro. Three months. We're just now telling folks."

Tie heard the smile in his voice.

"Aw, shit—you're gonna be a father! All the best to you two, that's great, man. Give Vanessa a hug and kiss for me."

"She'd like that. You know I still think she has a crush on you."

"Stop."

"Doesn't matter. I'm the one who knocked her up."

"Hey, look out for Meg for me, will you? Her husband's a big guy, but there are some bad people out there."

"You got it, man. I go near her apartment on my way to work."

"Thanks, man." He breathed a sigh of relief as he ended the call.

He was through with crunches, though in need of some sparring. Instead, he headed for one of the punching bags and imagined beating the shit out of it.

Chapter Twenty

Another Monday, last week of the semester, another week ahead to prove to herself, never mind others, that she was worthy of being a professor at the college. But this latest debacle, landing a student in the hospital while having any amount of alcohol in her system was still hard to live down. The circus had cooled down on social media, from Nette's report, but memories of the incident kept Laney up at night.

Not to mention memories of the fight with Tie. And knowing she wouldn't see him any time soon.

Walking down the path past the administration building, the sight before her arrested her steps. A group of students was on the front lawn, some sitting, some standing, but all of them holding some kind of sign. And, although just a few were facing her, she saw her name on the placards.

Keep Dr. Travers!
Dr. Travers is the ideal Sheffield prof.
Dr. Travers is essential to Sheffield!
We refuse to allow Dr. Travers to leave!

And, holding a bullhorn on the front steps was none other than Alex! Shy, reticent, blushing Alex.

For her? She tentatively approached the steps, smiling appreciatively at the students along the way. A round of applause rippled through the small crowd.

"Alex?" She looked at him and he blushed. "What's going on here? Why are the students doing this? Who organized it?"

Alex's pale face reddened. "I did, Dr. Travers, but a whole bunch of us readily agreed. You know, rumors go around, and it sounds like there's a chance your contract might not be renewed. We think that's unacceptable, because you're a... you're an awesome teacher, and that's why we're at the school. To be taught by really great teachers who care," he gushed.

"Alex," she whispered, noting others standing nearby, and not wanting to embarrass him. "I have to say I'm really proud of you. This took a lot of initiative. I mean, I'm beyond flattered and actually floored that you guys would do this, but I'm also impressed."

Alex blushed. "I don't know if you know, but Blaine— the kid you hit—is actually my brother."

Laney's mouth fell open. "Oh, my god, I'm so sorry. How's he doing?"

"He's okay. Just broken and bruised, but not really the first time. Well, it's never been this bad, but he'll recover. I just want you to know that I, we, don't blame you. It was an accident. My parents—big donors to the school, by the way—know that I've organized this, and they're in support." Alex looked Laney directly in the eyes, and Laney saw a sincerity she couldn't have dreamed of.

"They are?" *I have no idea why they would be...* It dawned on her. Alex. Her time and attention to him meant more to him than she ever would have guessed. "Thanks for that, Alex. It's good to hear that. But I am still very, very sorry for what happened."

Alex nodded. "We know." Alex laughed. "Honestly, I think Blaine is happy to have a concussion that gets him out of finals. And maybe he'll think twice before getting plastered."

Laney smiled sadly. She indicated the bullhorn. "May I?"

She accepted the bullhorn from Alex then thought better of it. She was a professor. She knew how to project her voice before a crowd, and she certainly didn't need to obnoxiously attract the attention of higher administration.

She walked to the center at the top of the steps. Again a smattering of applause. She recognized many faces and smiled, as they gave her a sense of well-being and made her feel more confident.

"I just want to say thank you to you all. I'm flattered and impressed that you would take the time to voice your support of me. I want you all to rest assured that I will remain dedicated to my work, especially my teaching, as long as I'm here."

"We want you to stay!" someone yelled out.

"I want to stay, too. But we'll see how it all works out. Believe me when I say that your voices have been heard loud and clear by me, and you give me confidence that I'll come out on the other end just fine!"

Enthusiastic applause.

"Yay!"

"You go, Dr. Travers!"

"Fenwright sucks!" one of her supporters said, referring to the name of the administration building.

Laney smiled at some of their comments.

"Now, as I promised, I am dedicated to my work. So I must leave you now. You've done more than enough. Thank you so much."

A smattering of applause.

As she walked down the steps in a daze, she wondered how on earth such positive energy had sprung up on her behalf. As worn down and guilty as she was feeling, the students represented an alternative view. She was appreciated, as a teacher and as a human being.

As she neared her building, she heard Alex on the bullhorn. "Justice for Dr. Travers! Hell no, she won't go!" She couldn't suppress a smile. She really couldn't judge a book by its cover.

"Wow, should we all clap for you?" Debbie greeted her as Laney entered the hallway to the psychology faculty offices. "You have quite the cheering section out there."

"Well"—Laney ignored the sarcasm in Debbie's voice— "I think I've received enough applause for the morning, thank you. And obviously it's more meaningful coming from the students."

Debbie gave her a long look and turned away. "Let's just hope they don't end up disappointed," she called over her shoulder.

Don't react, Laney. She's baiting you, as usual. Don't let anything spoil the positive energy you received this morning, you'll need to carry it through the day. The week. The month.

And then next semester.

She took a deep breath, forced a smile, and unlocked her office. "Time to get to it," she announced to no one in particular.

Her smile turned genuine. Tenure was desirable, but in any case this was her work. This was where she belonged.

LANEY HAD GONE back to turning off the radio at six thirty p.m. It had been too painful to hear Tie's voice, especially since he—of course—sounded unaffected by everything. Just because Laney could barely lecture after their fight—uh, breakup—didn't mean he couldn't be as sharp as ever. And, again, she needed the half hour back to compensate for her lack of concentration.

As much as she thought she wanted to drink away her grief, she refrained from her wine—she had begun to fall unforgivably behind at work, and it would be reflected in her student evaluations as well as her colleagues' opinions of her committee contributions. At this point in the semester, it could be a nightmare. And beyond, the implications for obtaining tenure were pretty clear. She simply could not risk being denied tenure. The job security that tenure provided would allow for the first real chance at stability Laney had in life.

Whatever. If she could just finish the semester and then be allowed to collapse thereafter, she'd have a solid deal with the universe.

"I MISS AALIYAH," Laney said, absentmindedly.

Nette glanced at her as she was driving. "The singer? The one who's been dead—may she rest in peace—for two decades? Where'd that come from?"

Laney snapped back to attention. "Oh, that's Tie's ringtone. 'At Your Best.'"

"Could you be any cheesier?"

Laney didn't take offense. That was Nette's way of trying to redirect Laney's emotions. Ever since she and Nette had mended ways she'd been careful not to trigger her. That essentially meant not mentioning "Black," "White," "race," or "Devin." Plus, Nette was trying to help.

"Well, you know, that was a coming of age song, and those always stay larger than life." Laney laughed it off.

"Right. Thanks to Smashmouth, I still think I'm an all-star."

"And you are." They bumped fists as Nette turned her Lexus into the parking lot of Nordstrom at Easton Town Center.

"I still think this is a waste of time," Laney whined. "You've worked corporate, you have wealth. I need to shop at Marshalls."

"I mean, Marshalls and TJ Maxx have their place; I'm not denying that. But we're professional women, and lord knows you stayed in school too long to have to compromise."

"But I actually like Marsh—"

"Plus, Nette knows the deal. This time of year has good sales on certain items as they begin to clear inventory."

"Whatever." Laney doubted that the days before Christmas were ideal for shopping and, besides, she wasn't in the mood to shop.

The semester was ending and she could wear the same outfit five days in a row as far as she was concerned. Just, others might notice and start asking questions. She already had too many people in her business. But she'd come along to humor Nette, and to make Nette believe she was successfully distracting Laney.

"Hello, Nenette!" a tall woman, with a platinum-blonde French roll, said. She was primly standing behind the Dior counter.

"Oh, hi, Olivia. Anything new you think I'd be interested in? You know I'm a M.A.C gal, but you also know I like to diversify…"

"Oh, one of the girls working the M.A.C counter today is kind of a… shall we say, an unpleasant person. You're better off at our counter today," she whispered with a conspiratorial smile.

Laney wandered off a bit, toward the jewelry counters. The flashes of diamonds, of course, caught her eye. She turned around to walk in the opposite direction. The last thing she needed to see right now were sparkly engagement rings and cute little holiday gift boxes "for her." She fought back tears. *Stop it, Laney. It was barely over three months, and that's counting the weeks you were apart!*

She could try to rationalize all she wanted. The length of

time didn't matter.

"Excuse me…"

She looked over her shoulder. A handsome man perhaps a couple of shades lighter than her, with gray eyes, was standing by one of the jewelry cases and looking at her. He reminded her of a young Jesse Williams, and, intrigued, she momentarily wondered if he was as woke as the celebrity.

"Hi. Do you mind helping me out for a second?"

Laney politely turned toward him. "Oh, I don't work here. There was a woman—"

"Pardon me. I mean, I didn't think you worked here. I just wanted to get your opinion on a couple of pieces." He smiled and raised his eyebrows questioningly.

Oh no, here we go. He's going to ask what type of ring he should get his soon-to-be-fianceé. Can't he see that I'm not wearing a ring? Why would I be interested? Still, at this point it would seem inauthentic for her to be off in a hurry, and his smile was as charming as they came, along with his captivating eyes.

"Sure." She walked over to stand by his side and was relieved to see that he wasn't standing in front of rings.

He indicated three gold earrings in a row. Very simple and elegant, although not something she would personally expect from a boyfriend at Christmastime. "Which of these three do you think would be most appreciated by a fifteen-year-old girl?"

Ah, that made more sense. She glanced up at him. "Your…"

"Niece."

"You can't go wrong with any of these, especially given she's your niece. Now, if she were your daughter, which wouldn't be possible—" She quickly sized him up, realizing he was probably several years younger than her. "You know, parents really ought not to guess when it comes to their teenage children. They'll always be wrong!"

They laughed, and his eyes lingered on her for a few seconds. He had a dimple that reminded her of Tie's, except on the other cheek.

"You have beautiful eyes," he said, looking back toward the earrings. He seemed a bit shy. For some reason, it tugged on Laney's sympathy.

She glanced back at the earrings. "Thank you. You know, that pair in the middle seem to have the more secure backs, so I would go with those. I have a box full of gold and silver earrings that have lost their mate but I can't allow myself to get rid of them."

He chuckled. "Thanks."

"Not a problem. Happy holidays." She turned to leave.

"Excuse me again."

She turned around, this time she was the one with raised eyebrows.

"I'm sorry, just I'd be kicking myself for the next few days if I didn't at least ask if you were single."

"Well, I…" *Guess he did notice I'm not wearing a ring.* "I'm sort of in a relationship, so, you know…"

He looked slightly deflated. "Sort of—yeah, no—totally get it. I just, you know…"

Nette sidled up to Laney, clearing her throat as discreetly

as Laney supposed she could.

"Oh, Nette, I was just helping this… gentleman… select earrings for his niece."

He looked from Laney to Nette. "Tell you what. Let me give you both my card. I'd love to hear from either of you." His eyes lingered on Laney. "Again, thanks."

"Again, no problem."

"What's up with the hottie?" Nette whispered rather loudly, when they were otherwise out of hearing distance.

"Not a thing. I told him I'm sort of in a relationship."

"What? Don't you know this is exactly what you need for distraction? Did you *see* him? No one said you had to move in with him. But a date… he is *not* hard on the eyes!" She looked back in the direction of the jewelry, although they were headed to women's clothing.

Laney sighed. "Then you call him. He gave us both his card." She looked at the small piece of paperboard. Clyde Turner, C.F.A., Lyons, Marshall & Dunbar.

"That was to save face, and you know it. Although I wouldn't be too proud to take your castoffs. Like going to a Kardashian thrift store."

Laney rolled her eyes. "Can we move on to something else? I'm not going to date anyone. Tie and I haven't discussed anything like that. We haven't officially broken up."

Nette paused from examining a green silk blouse and stared at Laney like she had fingers growing out of her head. "Oh no."

"I'm just saying… neither of us officially said it's over. Those words, like, 'it's the end'…" Her voice faded.

"Laney... this isn't good for you. You're either in or you're out. You made it sound hopeless. I thought... I think you two need to have a real talk. Like, soon. This ambiguous state isn't doing you any good."

Laney shook her head vigorously. "And you know what? Neither is this line of discussion. I'm done." She held her lips tight, knowing Nette would get the message.

But Nette was having a hard time keeping her mouth closed. After a lull, Laney cajoled Nette into trying on the silk blouse, partly so she could get a little mental space for a few minutes. "Oh, that would look so beautiful on you, with your auburn hair. It's such a gorgeous shade of green." *Oh... like Tie's eyes.* Shit. This was going to be a long holiday season.

Chapter Twenty-One

"GIRL, WHY ARE you trippin'? Ain't nobody worried about who you're dating! Trust me, as a group, sisters—at least the mature ones past college—are happy just to see a sister happily in a relationship. You know how hard it is, especially for professional women."

"But come on, Tracey. There's judgment. And, among our colleagues and students alike, there would be the questioning of my authenticity as a Black person and whether I can relate to being Black at all."

Tracey and Laney had gotten together for a binge fest of *Orange is the new Black*. She didn't usually see Tracey during the holiday break, so it was nice to have another girlfriend to hang with during what felt like a lonely period. Tracey's condo was nice and toasty, and had a sophisticated design that somehow still felt homey. They had a big bowl of popcorn between them. They were both in yoga or sweatpants and hoodies.

Tracey gaped at her. "You for real? Girl, first of all, the only judgment around here would be coming from the few Black men on campus, half of whom are with White women—no, strike that, Al is with a Filipino—and secondly, you're not teaching anything that would connect to African-

American culture, no matter who is teaching it. What the hell?

"And as far as I'm concerned, any woman with a natural is, by definition, not running scared from her heritage." She took a sip of her water. "Not that our sisters with relaxed hair *are*." She flipped her own soft keratin-straightened locks over her shoulder. "The only issue you should be concerning yourself with, with regard to this aspect of your *private* life, is whether the man respects you, and whether you have feelings for him. And vice versa. If the answers are affirmative, then go, you!" Another sip of water. "Do you know how many of us *wish* that were the case for us?" Tracey rolled her eyes. "But I'm not holding my breath. The online dating thing is just a breeding ground for pigs."

A little hyperbole there, but okay. Everything coming out of Tracey's mouth made so much sense. How did that happen? Laney was starting to feel better after hearing her assertions. She could trust Tracey. Her friend was so confident and well-respected by all their peers, regardless of background.

"Have you seen *Something New*?" Tracey paused the program, turning to Laney.

"What do you mean?"

"The movie. With Sanaa Lathan."

"No, I haven't seen her in a minute. Somehow I missed that one."

"Anyway, she fell in love with her White gardener, but had a really hard time accepting it because of the challenges that came along with it regarding race, and his slowness to understand. You remind me of her character. But she loved him, and love triumphs."

"In Hollywood? Of course. But let's be real. I have to consider tenure. Look who is on the committee." Laney was referring to Dante Michaels, head of African diaspora studies.

Tracey drew in a breath. "Dante would be hard-pressed to find something actual to hold against you. There's nothing. Nothing. His distaste for anyone's lifestyle can't be a factor. Think about it."

Laney had already given it a lot of thought. But, again, Tracey made it sound so simple and logical. Was it really? Had Laney really been boneheaded enough to fight Tie over some stupid politics that might not even exist?

"You still with me?" Tracey moved her head side to side, trying to catch Laney's eyes.

"Oh, yeah. I was just thinking."

"Of taking some time tomorrow to go get things straight with your man, I hope," Tracey demanded, nodding. "That lecher in your department would pose more of a problem than Dante. I should think Dante is invested in strengthening the numbers of faculty of color. You need to Go. Get. Your. Man."

Laney had to laugh at the firm decisiveness of her friend. "Yeah, maybe. But it won't be easy."

"Nothing worthwhile ever is. Listen, I'm not the psychologist here, so call me out if you have to, but are you sure this isn't all about something else? I mean, you're a sharp woman, Laney, and I know you're pre-tenure, but kicking your relationship with your dream man to the curb because of racial politics that might not even by at play… it just doesn't square."

Why did it always seem silly when others presented the situation to her? Could Tracey really not understand? Then again, maybe she *was* failing to articulate a big aspect of the problem that even she wasn't conscious of. She liked to think of herself as having good self-insight, but who made her the expert?

"You know you're making this hard, Tracey. You had me for a moment, but then you go throw this wrench in. What if I do have some deep-seated issue… maybe it's not wise to go running back until I figure that out."

"Oh please. In good relationships, you figure those things out together. You just have to give it a chance. Sure wish I had a chance." She threw a handful of popcorn into her mouth and resumed the program.

Now it was Laney's turn to give her friend an encouraging smile.

But she'd also need to leave enough encouragement in reserve for what she was about to do. She had to make it happen.

"IT'S NOT GOING to happen," Tie said, not looking Laney in the eye.

Laney had finally worked up the courage to walk into the station, catch Tie in his office and secure a moment with him. After a deep breath, she had proposed that they try to "start over fresh." Now the worst-case scenario was staring her in the face.

Her heartbeat increased and she felt a little dizzy. She rested an arm on his desk for support. Laney longed to have his beautiful eyes glued to her, adoringly as they used to be. What had she done? *It's not going to happen because of me. I lost my chance.*

"Tie, I understand that you're upset, and I'm sorry that I hurt you, but I've thought it over, talked it over, and now I see how foolish I'd been."

"Now you do. Or, at least you say you do. But what happens tomorrow when you encounter an essay about how White-men-Black-women relationships reenact an enslaved mentality? Or something? Are you strong enough to shrug that off? Are you able to take me to any function where there'll be a lot of Black folks?"

It stung that Tie was questioning her strength, one of the characteristics that he had first admired about her. She had created a real mess. "My strength hasn't gone anywhere. Believe it or not, it took all my strength to have that difficult conversation with you. The problem was, I guess I was exerting my strength in the wrong direction. Now I know what I want—I mean I always knew what I wanted, but now I think I know how to fight for it." Laney desperately hoped it was the right thing to say. She couldn't fill in the blanks with anything more convincing. She collapsed onto his sofa, suddenly deflated.

Now Tie looked at her. His jaw was like steel and his

eyes weren't their usual brilliant green but rather a stormy, tornado green. Laney knew what this look meant. She had seen it directed toward a restaurant patron at a nearby table who made a racist comment.

But now his look of indignation and outrage was meant for *her*. And it hurt. Hurt her that she had hurt him in any way that could be comparable…

Tie clenched and unclenched his fists. "I need you to leave, Laney. It's just not going to happen, and it doesn't make sense to draw this out. No screaming, no grabbing." He put his hands in the air. "You're free, as you wanted to be."

Screaming and grabbing? Yes, there had been screaming during their fight. It was a real thing.

Laney reluctantly stood up. "That's just it, Tie, I don't think I was asking to be free. At least, not from you."

Tie took a deep breath and closed his eyes. "Then what did you want from me, Laney? What were you asking for?" he said through clenched teeth.

"I… wanted…" Laney could not fill in the blanks.

She turned and tried to look at him but averted her glance given the storm ranging in his reopened eyes. She took a long, ragged breath in, walked out the door, and hurried down to her car before the tears came.

Chapter Twenty-Two

TIE ACHED ALL over. Having to confront Laney like that was one of the hardest things he'd ever had to do.

And it was exhausting. Despite that he was worried he wouldn't be able to stand strong if she ever came back to him, his anger had threatened to pour out of him like a tsunami. Obviously, he had contained a lot of emotion and had some to get off his chest.

But the pain he saw reflected in her big beautiful brown eyes—it was nearly more than he could bear, nearly broke him, nearly had him drawing her into his arms. But he held fast.

And he did mean everything he said, so it would be worthwhile for her to consider the answers to his questions. Whether she eventually did, and whether she still wanted him upon doing so, well, that was part of the gamble he had to make.

But he inexplicably felt less safe, and very uneasy. Had he let go of the one person who made him feel whole and good enough as he was? Or someone who, in the end, did not believe in his potential? During this period, when he was trying to get an enterprise off the ground, he needed as much support as he could get. And he needed to feel whole.

He'd made the right choice. He had to have. She had no faith in their relationship. In *them*.

LANEY STOPPED BY the liquor store on her way home from the studios. She selected a magnum of champagne and a big bottle of cheap vodka. Taste would be the least of her concerns tonight. No, tonight would be about celebrating her apparent single life. Screw couples. She could do whatever the hell she wanted to do now, without answering to anyone, without shopping for clothes to look anything but professional. *You know what? Tie's loss.* He couldn't give them a second chance? Then she couldn't give a damn. It sure wasn't worth crying over. Damn worth toasting with drinks, though! She thought about inviting Nette, but Nette might have a thing or two to say about her plan to get plastered over Tie, and horrified by the sheer amount of booze.

Well, one thing was for sure. She would not be trying to contact him anytime soon. His harsh words and stormy eyes were seared into her brain, and she couldn't bear the thought of hearing and seeing them again anytime soon. Or standing so close to him without being able to touch him, taste him, and smell him.

She'd get it together. If she could get off the floor. And stop crying into her hands.

After a while she stood up, looked in the mirror, and splashed cold water onto her red eyes. She felt sympathy for the dejected woman looking back at her, but she also felt a bit of anger. "You got yourself into this mess, all around. You and your half-baked brain." She yanked on her dark brown hair just to feel the pain and to give herself a jolt. She wound her hair and pinned it up with a couple of brown claw clips. She noted the female symbol drawn in the upper corner of her mirror in red lipstick. That was from her makeup session with Nette, long ago. Her first date with Tie. Woman power triumphs, Nette had said.

Triumphs, my ass.

TIE WAS SITTING on his couch with his head in his hands. Some of the studio execs had headed out for drinks after work but Tie declined to join them. He just wanted to get home and do exactly what he was doing. His mother had always said that he was entitled to self-pity parties, so long as they didn't last longer than an hour. Well, he was a grown man and had broken most of his childhood rules by now, so this might be yet another one of them.

Why did she have to return? Why did she put him in the excruciating position of saying no? Could she read the conflict in his eyes at all? Did she know how much he really wanted her? God, if she hadn't truly rejected him in the first place, sucked the light out of him, then she surely would reject him now. He had been brutal.

He went to grab a beer. Seeing none, he closed the stainless-steel fridge and took some scotch out of his cabinet, instead. Tonight's show must have sucked. Nobody had said anything, and he usually did an incredible job of compartmentalizing before going on air, but visions of Laney's shining, pleading eyes kept accosting him throughout the show.

He welcomed the warmth of the scotch and took the glass with him to finish his pity party on the couch. He scrolled through photos of her on his phone, photos of them together, candid shots where she was not expecting him to capture her and diamond-precious shots that showed her illuminating smile. Which he just *had* to see again. This wonderful woman, though he did not mind sharing with her students, her friends, and even just spectators on the street, was his. Laney was his. But he had let her go.

He was looking at a selfie of the two of them from a Halloween party and wondered, for the umpteenth time, how she had spent Christmas and whether she had plans for the new year. A new year without him.

Chapter Twenty-Three

I T WAS DURING one of those states, when one awakens from an intense dream they cannot recall but feels a fundamental shift in consciousness, that Laney had a realization.

It was simple. As plain as day.

She didn't want to live in a world in which her love and happiness would not be welcome.

And this was in her control. She would simply block those people from her life. If she couldn't excise them, then she would promptly excuse herself and go elsewhere. Why would she want to stay in an emotional vacuum to please others?

Why hadn't she seen this sooner? Too many trees? Too much PhD?

Nette was always going on about doing away with toxic energy and toxic people; surely one could do away with a toxic environment. If the environment was really toxic. Either make changes to the environment, her relationship to the environment, or transfer to a new environment altogether.

She sat down at her computer to write down her thoughts, lest she forgot them when she was completely lucid. Before she returned to her "senses."

The first bit of writing felt so cathartic, Laney began writing every day, feeling more conviction about the beauty of her relationship—or potential relationship—after every entry. Thinking she couldn't possibly be the only one dealing with this problem, she decided to start a blog, "Transcendent Colors." She spent the rest of winter break writing her blog, preparing for classes, and willing herself to feel better.

It seemed to be working. She felt new. A great way to start a new year.

To add to her sense of fresh starts, she heard from Lola, who was finally in Narcotics Anonymous. If Lola could improve, surely Laney could.

And she started with the college transitional program, getting it in shape to present to their colleagues.

She had lunch with Tracey off campus, at a swanky downtown restaurant that served local foods. Over hearty gourd and root vegetable stew, they celebrated their achievement. As they toasted their plan with champagne, Laney considered the fact that many of the components of their proposed program came from ideas born from her work with Tie on his program.

She and Tie had been truly accomplishing goals together. All this time. Again, Laney had missed the forest for the trees.

"Well, girl, I'm proud of you. And big up to you for that blog. Cheers to your voice! Where did your clarity come from?" Tracey pulled her from her thoughts.

"I just realized that what I had with Tie was worth more than staying at an institution that would give me tenure but deny me the potential for love."

Tracey's eyes widened and she raised her flute again. "To knowing what you *really* want."

Laney clinked her glass. Yes, it was true. No one could call her a sellout now. Not even herself.

Chapter Twenty-Four

S PRING SEMESTER CLASSES were starting on Monday, but thank goodness Laney didn't have to teach until the day after. Although she'd been preparing for classes, she barely had her syllabi up and running because at the last minute her concentration became poorer than ever. Had she overdone it with all her thinking and writing? Was Nette undeniably right? Did she have ADHD?

Maybe it was Tie. Everything about the new year seemed on track except... Tie was no longer in her life.

She had always been a strong, independent woman. So why couldn't she exist properly without a man?

It's not about "a man." It's about Tie. She couldn't exist normally without him. He was a missing piece of her, and she could not figure out how to fill the void. The blog helped, but it wasn't enough. If he could just give her a second chance, she could convince him that she was truly ready for him. For them.

How was he doing it? She occasionally eavesdropped in on the radio program and his voice seemed as steady and colorful as ever. How did he manage, when she sometimes felt like a wreck lately? Professionally, she would have to get her act together. There was no excuse for otherwise at the beginning of the semester. She'd come this far.

She thought about calling Nette to see whether she wanted to work together this morning. It had been a long time since she needed a "work buddy," but there was no shame in admitting to her best friend her hard time keeping focused. Plus, Nette already knew she was a mess.

IT HAPPENED AROUND ten thirty p.m. the night before, according to Nette. At least, that was when it had entered her feed.

A brief video of Laney on stage as Flower, the naughty fairy had somehow gotten into the hands of a malicious person. She stared at the clip Nette forwarded to her, though she wished she hadn't seen it. She was unmistakably a stripper. The pole was even in the background. She looked younger and probably sexier, but it was still *her*. At least her double-D breasts were not yet bare in the photo. But they might as well have been. As far as she was concerned, she was nude and in full display for anyone with the slightest imagination. Who did this to her? And why? She would probably never find out. The important thing now was damage control, which... how did one proceed with damage control once something let loose on social media?

She groaned. She was fucked. Undoubtedly, this would reach at least one of Sheffield's students, and many of her colleagues were connected to students. If it had come through Nette's feed, posted by who knew, it had come close enough to create momentum in Laney's social space. All it took was one person. Perhaps it would not have been quite as bad if the caption hadn't read, "Naughty prof, give me private lessons!"

No. It would still be a nightmare. She had been outed.

She couldn't recall ever feeling so mortified in all her life. Her mouth was dry and she felt faint. She walked away from the standing desk in her home office and took a seat in her ergonomic desk chair. She put her head in her hands. How was she going to be able to show her face again? What would everyone think of her? Thank goodness it was a Saturday. She could hide all weekend.

The college! It was affiliated with a church, not quite a Christian school but nonsecular nonetheless. If the hiring committee had known of her past, there was little chance they would have hired her. Who needed that type of scandal at an otherwise modest college? *And this is on the heels of my hitting Blaine, for god's sake!*

But they couldn't fire her over this, could they? Although, surely this was more of a character issue than accidentally hitting a student—in the absence of an OVI citation. Oh, who knew what administration and committee members would make of anything! *Don't ask, don't tell.* Yes, that would be her motto. But there could be a lot of buzz, even among people who hadn't seen it. Word of mouth was proof enough. Would some people, with big mouths like Debbie or Gina, broadcast it for all?

Broadcast! Tie!

Oh no. She hadn't had a chance to tell him of this aspect

of her past. If he saw this before she could explain it to him, would he think she'd intentionally withheld a relevant secret from him? Would it be a deal breaker forever? Either way, she had to find out. She didn't want to take chances. Plus, it was only fair that he be warned about the video for his own sake. They did have, after all, a past connection. She had to see him as soon as possible.

TIE HAD BEEN surprised to receive a phone call from Laney, and astounded that she wanted to see him. Furthermore, her tone sounded conciliatory and urgent, but not desperate or hopeful. So, it didn't sound like an attempt to make up. But the emergency in her voice made Tie agree to see her. And, if he were honest with himself, he really just wanted to lay eyes on her. He ached for her.

They were to meet at a Starbucks downtown. *This is not a date*, he kept reminding himself—they were still in a breakup. But he had been feeling like half his soul was missing since the night of the gala. Granted, he was still trying to compensate for the disaster she had created with her charity event gaffe, but his anger and humiliation couldn't override the desire he had to be with her.

He simply couldn't stop thinking of her. Her lovely face, dark tresses, sharp wit and gentle touch. Her smell, her smile, and her laughter. He hadn't realized her laugh had become one of his most favorite sounds in the world. If he had a playlist of Laney sounds, her laugh would figure prominently on it. And her lecture voice, which she occasionally slipped into when they were discussing current events. She sounded as wise as she was. The playlist would, of course, be incomplete without some other sounds he tried not to think about, as sex should be the furthest thing from his mind.

It wasn't a workday, so she wasn't wearing her uniform of blazer and pants. She wore snug jeans, tall boots, and a big baby-blue angora sweater. Her hair was loose. She looked like she'd lost a little weight, but her curves were still obvious. She looked like a million bucks. His heart quickened as she spotted him and headed toward the table. She was looking around, eyes wide. She seemed to be looking for someone. Or making sure someone was not there.

It was an awkward greeting. There was no kiss, no hug, not even a handshake.

Laney simply nodded at him. "Tie."

And he nodded back. "Laney."

He waited for her to get her black coffee and return to sit across from him. He watched every move she made, not knowing when he would see her again. He had to touch her.

She bit her lip and looked down at the table. He had the urge to smooth the worry lines from her forehead. She looked so despondent.

Finally, she took a deep breath and looked at him. "I'm guessing you haven't seen it yet, but there is a video of me going around online."

He cocked his head.

"When I was in college, in order to help me pay for expenses, I danced. You know, *danced*."

He had no idea where the conversation was going, and his confusion must have shown on his face.

She looked away, sighed, then looked back at him. "Exotic dancing, Tie. I was a stripper."

He didn't even blink as he lost himself in Laney's luscious eyes. Perhaps it took a moment for her words to register, but he still did not react as surprised as he would have expected. She had a hold on him; his heart was wide open at the moment.

Finally, his eyebrows lifted. "Well, how was that for you, baby? Dancing during those days. How did you feel about it?"

He saw a flicker of emotion cross her face. He hadn't meant to let "baby" slip out.

Her eyes enlarged as she looked at him with surprise. "I-I still don't know. On stage I felt in charge, powerful. Offstage… I tried not to think about it. I guess I've tried not to think about it since I quit. Past is past, thank god." She rubbed her arm. "At least, I was hoping the past stayed in the past. But I don't regret using my paycheck and tips to pay for school!"

"You're a resourceful genius." He smiled. "I was thinking about that, Laney, how resourceful and resilient you and I are as individuals… we could probably be a dynamic duo if we put our 'powers' together." He studied her for her reaction.

She looked confused. "You're taking this awfully well, Tie. Do you get what I said?"

"Look, I won't deny being a wee bit jealous that so many

other men got to ogle the body—the woman—I've adored, but if you hadn't taken the steps you did, we'd not have met. And… I am glad that we met. As long as you're okay with your past, I am." He was surprised that she was bothering to tell him any of this now.

Laney returned his smile. "That's one way to look at it. The important thing is, you're not judging me."

Tie scowled. "Judging? Laney, I admire everything about you. Always have. I doubt I could ever learn anything that would change that." He reached across the table and wrapped one of her soft ringlets around his long finger and tugged gently.

Laney closed her eyes momentarily and a small smile appeared on her face.

Her eyes snapped open.

She pulled back and shook her head. "Oh, god. But you don't understand the worst part. You have this way of making me forget… Listen, Tie. This is serious."

Her grave tone sent shivers down his spine and made the hairs on his forearms stand on edge. He leaned forward even more and gave her a look he hoped conveyed he was taking this all very seriously, and waited for her to continue.

She gave a slight nod and looked down. She took a napkin from the table and smoothed it on her lap. "The video of me reached Nette's account around ten p.m. I haven't talked to Tracey or anyone else about it yet, but there's a good bet that someone on campus has seen it by now. After all, Nette is an instructor."

He was silent, not making sense of what she was saying.

Then, when he connected the dots, his hand flew to his mouth. Video! *Oh, Laney!* He wasn't sure what to say without minimizing the situation while trying to be supportive and reassuring.

"Were you... at all clothed?"

Her eyes finally met his. She seemed to take a breath of relief. It must have taken some doing to get that much off her chest. "Barely, but yes. It will be clear to anyone that I was a stripper. And if there were a speck of doubt, the pole in the background helps to provide context. They'll recognize me for sure. I'm an inveterate performer! First as a stripper, now as a professor."

"And it's clearly you?" Hopefully, the footage, which had to be old, was grainy and blurry.

She nodded. Yes, of course folks could tell. Laney's distinctive beauty was not easily confused with another. If the clip captured her soulful eyes, that alone was a wrap.

"I could just hang myself from that pole now." Her voice broke and she leaned forward and put her face in her hands.

He'd never heard such an expression of hopelessness coming from her lips, and he didn't doubt that their breakup was not helping the situation.

He leaned over and stroked her soft hair. "Honey. Honey. This will blow over. It's in your past. It's not who you are. It's a part of your history. You have nothing to be ashamed of."

When she looked up there were unshed tears in her eyes and she looked at him gratefully. "You're gracious to say that, but you and I both know that this will have repercussions. And"—some tears began to fall—"the reason I needed to speak with you as soon as possible is that I want you to be able to get ahead of the story, as they say in your business. I'm so sorry to do this to you *again*, Tie!"

Suddenly, the larger parts started coming together. Her gaffe at the gala. Her accident involving alcohol—OVI or not, it was also on social media. And now this. Within the span of a few weeks, she appeared to have become a train wreck. But she wasn't a mess—he knew this without a doubt. Though he didn't necessarily understand it all, he knew the backstories. Yet that was knowledge—and motivation—the public did not have.

He could see the headlines—

Tie Steven's former lady friend's latest secret!

Professor and NPR host sweetheart strips their love life bare!

"Tie?" She sniffled a little.

"Hmmm. Oh, nothing. I was just… thinking… wondering how far this… news… could spread."

She nodded and worry lines deepened in her forehead. "You're worried, and you have every cause to be. Please tell me if there's anything I can do to help with damage control, Tie. Everything you're trying to do is important, and I, I—"

She took a long sip of coffee.

He sighed, leaned back in his chair, and ran his fingers through his hair. Shit. What more was there to say? As much as he wanted to hold her, stroke her, ultimately make love to her, they weren't ready for that kind of intimacy, if they ever would be. And he suspected Laney suggested a coffee shop as a way to avoid being completely alone with him despite her qualms about being seen in public with him.

Why hadn't she told him about her stripper days sooner? Not that the knowledge would have changed anything, but maybe…

Maybe nothing.

Chapter Twenty-Five

LANEY AND NETTE were walking around the indoor track at the college. This was one of the activities they planned to regularly engage in now that a fresh semester was upon them. Laney had tried to ditch day one because she had no desire to be on campus proper sooner than she needed to be. Nette crossly told Laney on the phone that if she did not join her on the track, she would find someone else to become her new bestie, with whom she would walk happily ever after. Laney couldn't deal with the melodrama, and Nette's real concern was in making sure that Laney didn't curl up in a ball and stay there.

Now that they were walking, she had to admit that her spirits were a bit lifted. That wasn't saying too much, but Laney needed every bit of help she could get at the moment.

As usual, Nette looked the part. She was wearing Lululemon leggings that somehow didn't look indecent on her and a fuchsia hoodie covering a Lycra top. Laney had shown up in sweatpants and a sweatshirt. She had no idea what people were wearing in the gym these days.

Nette took a sip of her water out of a bottle that matched her hoodie. "So you haven't mentioned it."

Laney remained silent, although she knew full well what

"it" was.

"You know I'm not interested in gossip—when it comes to you. I just want to know how you're feeling about it, how you're dealing with it."

Laney stopped to catch her breath. It had been hard enough to maintain light conversation as they began their walk, since Laney was so out of shape. This line of conversation required a deep breath and probably longer sentences.

"I don't know, Nette. I'll have to handle things as they come along. Or as they blow up. I don't know what else to do."

Nette grabbed her by the arm and led her forward on the track. "First of all, we're gonna keep walking. Self-care should be top priority for you right now, for so many reasons. Exercise is great all around. And standing at your standing desk doesn't count as exercise."

"See, I kinda thought it did."

"No, honey. And, second, we talk frankly about it."

She remained quiet. Thank god Nette had known about her background before her best friend laid eyes on the video. This was one time she wouldn't have to explain, one fewer person she would have to confess to.

"Do you want to know what's going around on social media or what?" Nette asked gently.

Another deep breath.

"No, not at all. But... I need to arm myself before I walk into classes tomorrow. I'm meeting my classes for the first time, for god's sake." This was so unfair.

"I agree, hon. Well, as you might expect, there's quite a

mix of reactions. The video has landed into the feeds of some students, and I assume some are reposting and/or commenting, but I can only tell from the students I follow or I'm friends with. It's amazing how much nerve some students have. They must have one hundred percent confidence that they'll never have a class with you.

"But I've noticed in some comments students are defending you, saying that it's your past, declaring that it's your right to do what you want with your body, and so forth. One person even questioned whether it's really you. And, of course"—she glanced at Laney—"there are the idiots who put one and one together and get twenty-four. So, you drink and you used to be an exotic dancer, therefore you must be the biggest party girl on campus."

None of this sounded worse than what had been swirling about in her imagination, so Laney experienced the tiniest bit of relief.

"Lots of flattering comments about your figure."

"I don't need to hear that. I get enough of that on Ratemyprofessor.com."

"Sorry. I wasn't thinking. So how are you feeling?"

"Hot as hell." Laney wiped sweat from her brow with her sleeve.

"You know what I mean. How do you feel about going in tomorrow?"

"A little better, thanks to your report. It actually sounds less horrible than I'd imagined. You don't want to know what's gone on inside my head. But, of course, I'm still dreading this. It sucks, because I had been looking forward to these classes, too."

"You can still look forward to them! This will blow over in ten minutes. You know from day one students are only concerned about their grades."

"That's what Tracey said about the accident debacle."

"Tracey the friendly ghost?"

"Okay! I'll have the three of us meet up for dinner one night so that you each can start believing the other person exists."

"You really are sweating. This is when you take off your sweatshirt. That's why I wear a zip-up hoodie. It's easier to remove."

Laney was about to pull up her sweatshirt when she remembered that she had on only a tank top beneath. Shoot. And of course there were students in the gym—mostly males—practicing basketball shots and running the outside lanes of the track. "No can do. I'm wearing only a tank top under here, which I wouldn't sport on campus anyway, but given the circumstances…"

"Of course. Okay, from now on, a light, short-sleeved top and a hoodie, capisce?"

"Yes, ma'am. But I'm going to have to wrap it up now before I pass out."

"And bring water, Laney!"

"Yes, yes. T-shirt and water. Now let's get going so that I can spend the next two hours trying to figure out which of my outfits makes me look most matronly. I have to set a certain tone tomorrow."

"Matronly? Oh, dear god. Are we that close to the edge?"

LANEY THOUGHT ABOUT Tie as she walked to campus. Their last encounter had been interesting. She hadn't processed it until now, because of all the worry around the stripper video, but she was starting to identify a feeling she hadn't noticed initially. Something like... hope? No way. Just because Tie had been empathetic and caring toward her didn't mean that they were getting back together. That was who Tie was. He was a wonderful, special man that any woman would be lucky to have by her side. The fact that he'd treated Laney with such kindness did not mean he wanted her, needed her, ached for her in the ways she had for him. She tried to squelch the unfamiliar feeling but part of it stayed in her consciousness, like a faint but unmistakable part of a constellation, a twinkle that meant *something*.

Out of the corner of her eye, she noticed the periodic stares of students and overheard their muffled conversations. Yes, some of them had definitely either come across the video or heard about it from a peer. But she could pull this off. *You've got this.* She steadied herself and pulled herself a little taller before she walked onto the floor of her department.

If Debbie and her lewd husband were not present, things might not have to be so unpleasant this morning. But, of course, they were there. Indeed, for once Debbie was standing in the doorway to her husband's office.

"Well! Good morning to our celebrity! Aren't you just full of surprises?"

Jeff made no attempt to hide the gleam in his eye and slimy grin as he looked Laney up and down. "I knew she had a story, that one." He pointed at Laney.

Laney ignored them both as she unlocked her door and headed into her office. He could look her up and down all day, but he'd eventually get bored. She was wearing a cream blouse buttoned to the top under a buttoned-up navy blazer, and her poly/cotton pants weren't particularly flattering to her figure. She had every intention of setting an "about business" tone in the classroom that would have her students quickly forgetting about stripper videos. Finally complete, her syllabi alone should keep them occupied for a while.

Debbie followed her into the office. "You do know that our colleagues have seen the video, too?"

Yeah, Laney figured as much. Again, she had imagined the worst. She didn't have time to hear the report from a Chatty-Cathy doll. "Debbie, I'm sorry, but I really have a lot to do before my first class, so you're going to have to excuse me." With that she turned away and unpacked her laptop, leaving Debbie standing disappointed at the door.

After her last class, Laney collapsed in her chair with an audible sigh of relief. Yes, some whispering and very curious stares, even some smirks and note passing, but not so different from the first day of class in any given semester. She did note a bit more traffic than usual passing her office and wondered if it was somehow related to her "celebrity," but she refused to take that thought further.

Instead, a smile actually spread across her face as a thought occurred to her. Finally! She would see if she could contact Tracey and Nette and arrange for the three of them to have dinner this evening. Yes, tomorrow was a workday but she had to acknowledge having gotten through this day. Tracey might not even know about the video, so she might as well get reeled in. Laney needed all the support she could get. And if there was anything else she wanted to know, well, there was Nette.

She picked up her phone, maintaining an authentic smile for the first time in days.

Chapter Twenty-Six

CHERYL BUMPED INTO Tie in the station kitchen.

"Tie! Good to see you. Your show's been going very well, as always. We really lucked out with you."

"Oh, thanks, Cheryl. As you know, I can't take all the credit. Lot of staff working with me."

"Yeah." She nodded, her mind apparently already somewhere else. Looking around the empty room, she said quietly, "Did you know there's a video of your—"

"Yes." He cut her off. "She was practically a child then."

"She looked pretty young. I only know about it because one of our interns posted it. A Sheffield student, I think. How is she taking it?"

Tie's mouth was open but he had no words. This was an unfamiliar position for him, as he'd learned to be a fast thinker on his feet and thus was always able to maintain conversation. "Uh, I... don't..."

"I'm sorry. It was rude of me to put you on the spot. I don't know if you're even still seeing—I mean, you're not her spokesperson, are you?" She gave an awkward laugh. "Well, good luck with tonight's show. I'm sure it'll be fantastic, as usual." She said this last sentence in a rush on her way out of the room.

Tie poured coffee into his WYQT membership mug. Yes, no doubt folks would automatically link Tie to the video if they had any knowledge of their relationship. Of course, this included many of his donors and a good number of his colleagues. This just as the fallout from the gala had pretty much cleared up thanks to lots of tap dancing and impromptu speeches on Tie's part. He had, by now, developed a certain eloquence on subjects of social justice.

Perhaps this video wasn't as bad, at least as far as his donors and program was concerned. The two weren't at all related, stripping and a financial literacy camp. It could be tied to a notion that he exploited women, but at this point that was a stretch. Of course, some people were still looking for those dots to connect. But, thus far, there had been no email queries or phone calls. He might just skate past this one.

How was Laney managing it all? How would this affect her job? To be held to account for choices when one was barely an adult... it did not seem fair. But myriad standards existed for gauging one's character.

He did know Laney's character was composed of kindness and caring, a deep appreciation for humanity, and other attractive qualities he had immediately been reminded of when they met two days ago. He wished he had the chance to be with her and witness the ways in which her character would expand and develop over time.

Meanwhile, he had made great strides in reinforcing the prospect of piloting the camp that coming summer. He had plenty of money as a down payment on renting the ideal space, just outside of the town center. He had funds to cover transportation for students who otherwise would not be able to make it to the three-week daily camp. He had funds to cover prospective field trips including an elaborate one to the Bureau of Engraving and Printing, which would involve overnight accommodations. He was still working on funds needed to fully cover payment to several camp counselors whom he would be training himself. He felt confident about a couple of the grants they had submitted.

So this training was probably the closest he was ever going to get to teaching, since money management seminars would not count, at least in his father's eyes. *You'll have to deal with that, Dad. Might not be good enough for you, but I think it just might be good enough for me.*

Craig's admonition, that it would not attract teens no matter the lack of cost stayed in his head. It was a good thing to keep in mind, because he would need to think about how to market the camp. If, in the final analysis, the marketing proved *too* successful, he would have to develop a lottery system for selecting kids for the camp. That would be a good problem.

But, after a lot of thought and soul-searching, there was one more thing he wanted to do. Had to do. He was tired of denying that his lack of formal education was a part of who he was. That if he'd finished school and gone down the business route he was headed or even the academic, law, or medical route his father desired, he probably would not have developed such a consciousness for personal finances.

He'd felt whole the moment Laney embraced his dropout status as just another part of his story, an aspect of what made him interesting. If anyone's opinion mattered, it was hers. He'd been making a favorable impression on her long before they actually met. She seemed mesmerized when he shared his expertise. Her fondness for him seemed unhindered by anything she learned about him, including his lack of a degree.

So, one day on air, after a particularly lively debate between two economists on the impending burst of an apparently existing bubble, Tie took a deep breath, paused, and spoke from his heart to his listeners.

"I've been in some of your lives for nearly three years now, and I'm sure more than once you've wondered about my background. I might sound smart and well read, and I don't deny either. But I actually never finished my college education. That's right. I'm a college dropout. University of Wisconsin, go Badgers. Anyway, the primary reason I'm sharing this with you is to let you know what motivated my interest in financial literacy and the youth camp I'm piloting this summer.

"Believe me, I had to learn rather quickly how to make money and then make my money work for me, not against me, not having a college education. It was entirely possible, but many of my initial steps were guided by the lessons on finances my parents instilled in me when I was young. My father broke down economic language into knowledge I could comprehend, and the rest, as they say, is history. So there it is, folks. Tie Stevens is a college dropout, but a successful college dropout. Now, let me be clear. I'm not promoting dropping out of college. That was a personal decision that fit me at the time. For most Americans, a college degree still remains essential. That's my two cents to add to the economy. Telling it like it is! Back with you tomorrow, everybody!"

Two cents of the invaluable worth you brought to my life, Laney.

Chapter Twenty-Seven

L ANEY HESITATED, DIALING his number then immediately hanging up about eight times before she finally let it ring through on the other end.

"Tie?"

"Hi, Laney." Laney couldn't figure out whether he sounded surprised, curious, pleased... but she took comfort in the fact that it wasn't a negative reaction.

Encouraged, she continued. "First, I want to tell you that I heard you on your program the other day, talking about not having completed college."

"That I was a dropout, yes."

"Well, yes. And it reminded me of what you'd said in Starbucks when we last met." She took a breath. "About how we're both resilient people and how we'd make a great team." Her voice shook a little on "team." She was making herself vulnerable here.

"Yes, I remember very well. I meant it." Now he sounded excited.

Encouraged, she tentatively smiled. "Well, I agree with you. And we've both independently decided to start programs to help other people develop resilience. Young people. I didn't fully realize it at the time, but I was picking up some helpful information from just being around you. You know, for this program I'm doing with Tracey."

"Yes, I know." The excitement was still there.

"Um… just tossing this out, but maybe we could help each other, you know, in further developing our ideas? I was thinking just a meeting sometime between the two of us. I mean, or Tracey could join us if you think that's better," she hurriedly added. She quickly realized his rejecting the two of them would be less painful than his rejecting just her.

"That's a really great idea, Laney." The excitement in his voice was replaced by rich contentment. "I'd be honored to help out, and I'd really benefit from finding out more about what you're thinking about the needs of incoming college students. Yeah, the two of us getting together sounds like a terrific idea." He delicately left out Tracey.

Laney's heart fluttered and her limbs relaxed. She would be seeing him again. Yes, they'd be talking business, but he would probably be inches away from her. She'd be able to feel his silky voice caressing her, his eyes would lock with hers on occasion, she'd smell his utopic scent, and if she reached over a little, she could… she blinked out of her thoughts, remembering she still had her fantasy lover on the line. "Awesome. Great."

There was a pause. Laney's heart flutters increased in intensity. Then both spoke at the same time.

"So, over coffee, you think?"

"Um, where would you like to—"

Tie laughed. "Right. Coffee sounds good. Um… I guess you'd like to meet in a coffee shop?"

Laney hesitated. She'd *like* to meet at his home, where they could cuddle together after a hot cup of coffee. But she dared not say it. Besides, he was probably bringing up a coffee shop because that was what *he* wanted. And they were, after all, still broken up. Maybe moving toward a friendship, but no longer lovers.

Her heart sank a little, but then she remembered she would still be seeing him. "Yes," she responded brightly. "That sounds great."

Tie took a long breath. "Good. I'm looking forward to this. And seeing you."

And she reached the next stop on the heart roller coaster—elated singing.

LATE IN THE morning, Laney opened the door to the local coffee shop owned in part by the sustainability program on campus. It had a wide selection of fair-trade organic coffees and teas available, and students served as the baristas. Given that Laney had been to this shop countless times, the butterflies crowding her stomach seemed out of place. And her hands were slightly sweaty as she pushed open the door.

She wasn't sure how this reunion would go. There wasn't the same sense of urgent business and emotionality that accompanied their last encounter. Should she act professional? Like a casual friend? Oh, she'd just have to go with whatever flow emerged. They'd had a relatively easy conversation on the phone. There was no reason to expect any worse now.

She wore a casual pink knit top with a boat neckline and a pair of cream-colored pants with some stretch to them. That hadn't been too hard to choose. Now she just needed to sit with the man for whom she had intense feelings and pretend that all was business as usual.

She walked in and immediately recognized one of her former students working the counter. She also saw a neuroscientist colleague on a laptop in the corner. She had been so self-conscious initially, having Tie on campus. How silly that had been.

She was so consumed with these thoughts she nearly missed Tie's wave.

"Oh, Tie! How are you?" She hurried over to… shake his hand.

Awkward, but he wasn't making any move and it seemed like the right thing to do. Each went to pull out her seat at the same time and laughed goodnaturedly about it.

"So," she said, breathlessly, "I hope you weren't waiting long."

"Nah. I arrived a little early and did a little walking around campus, since I haven't had much chance before. Pretty place."

"It is. One of the things that charmed me." She felt shy looking at him and so averted her eyes a little.

"Well, you look quite lovely, as usual."

"Thanks. Well, shall we get down to business?" She felt awkward and wanted to focus on something that provided her with firm footing. The program she and Tracey had spent hours sketching out would ground her when his eyes or an accidental touch might send her flying. Although part of her wanted that, to fly.

"Right." He pulled a thick binder out of his knapsack.

His gaze was on her face. When she dared to look at him, she noticed his parted lips and darkened eyes. She had seen that look before, and it flustered her. It reminded her of the last time they had made love, and the feeling of completeness—to the point of bursting—that accompanied it. That feeling she missed so painfully. Physically, emotionally.

It's just a work meeting, Laney.

"So," she began, "I figure we have a lot to gain from your knowledge of financial management in general, but specifically as it applies to incoming college students. Now, these are students who would have already selected their way of financing their first year of college, but our program can help them in determining what's best for them in the future. In college and beyond. You know, talk about the jobs that are available on campus—some that aren't advertised to all students—the dangers of credit cards, lots of time on interest and interest rates and so forth. Even savings. I've been advising students for a few years now—academically, but as I get to know them we talk about their lives in general. So many of them seem so lost when it comes to this stuff. What else do you think we should be expecting our students to need help with by the time they reach us?"

He stared at her a moment more. Had he heard anything she'd said? If he remained silent one second more Laney would lose her composure. Her hands were already trem-

bling and her question was at a higher pitch than sounded
natural.

"Well, it's already helpful to know that they're generally
lacking that practical information when they get to college.
That's the knowledge we'll work on building, and actually
putting into practice. The schools require students to pass a
financial literacy class before they graduate, but apparently
it's not enough. And a program like mine will only help
some youth, so college programs like yours are still going to
be very important."

He had heard her.

"Thank you." *For the encouragement and also for saving
me from begging you to come back to me!* "And we've gotten
enthusiastic green lights from the administration and likely
some support from other offices so, once Tracey and I
implement the program, we won't necessarily have to run it."

He nodded. "Sort of the same situation on my end.
Okay, so let's look at our respective plans and make notes."

She smiled. So far, so good.

An hour later, she felt good. She'd moved ahead on a
program that would help incoming underrepresented
students, mostly minority. And there were no awkward
moments, except when she and Tie accidentally touched
hands or met eyes and she could not control the electric
warmth that spread through her, as before. But she had not
lost her head.

"Thank you, Tie. This was helpful."

"The help was mutual." He sat back with his second cup
of coffee in hand and looked at her.

She was swept with the same sense of pride whenever he used to look at her like she'd said the wisest thing he'd ever heard. When he adored her.

"We could make a good team."

We. She smiled and looked down. "Excuse me."

His eyes were on her as she walked toward the counter. It made her self-conscious, and she hoped she was walking normally in spite of her hyperawareness.

"Hi, Josie."

"Oh, hi, Dr. Travers! What can I get for you?"

"Gee, what do you recommend? Any specials today?"

"Well, we're really excited about one of our original roasts that we've just developed…"

Laney listened to the endless possibilities that the world of coffee had evolved into and, as usual, felt overwhelmed. But… she also still felt that sense of accomplishment that was hard to come by lately, so she thought she'd celebrate by trying something new.

"All sounds good. Why don't I try that vanilla latte? What was it, the spirit latte?"

"Mmm-hmm." Josie rang her up and Laney handed over her ID/payment card.

She took a quick look over her shoulder as Josie prepared her coffee, and Tie was indeed staring at her butt, a small smile playing on his face. His eyes lifted to meet hers, and if he felt like he'd been caught in the act, he certainly didn't show any concern about it.

"Here you go, Dr. Travers. Enjoy the rest of your day."

"You too, Josie."

"So… no black coffee?" He had a small, amused smile.

"No. I thought I'd step out of my comfort zone for once. And so far"—she sipped her latte—"I've been rewarded."

He nodded, his eyes crinkled at the sides as he eyed at her with a curious look.

"Well, I'm sure you have to get to the studio…"

"I do. But, Laney…" He took a deep breath. "Can we do this again sometime soon? And maybe without all the notes?"

Now his look of amusement/curiosity was replaced by… was that hope? Or even pleading?

She hesitated. Her gut told her that the answer was yes! And her head argued a little, but she ruled that it was only habit. "Yes. I think that would be good."

Unspoken words, but when they met each other's gaze, she knew what the next meeting would be about. As she allowed herself to bathe luxuriously in his gold-flecked, incandescent eyes, she couldn't help but hope these unspoken words of adoration would be the first of many, many to come.

As they parted, she went to shake his hand again, but he staved it off with a tender, lingering kiss on her cheek, tantalizingly close to her lips. She stood there long after, touching the place where he'd kissed her and let the subconscious glimmer of hope resurface again.

Chapter Twenty-Eight

"HI, SHARON." LANEY sat down opposite the provost and waited for the latter to remove her readers.

"Elaine. We meet again." Sharon had a smug smile on her face.

Laney wondered how that fit into context. She quickly decided it didn't matter, and her own genuine smile stayed on her face. It was nearly spring, a crisp beautiful morning, spring break was upon them, and she was looking forward to seeing Tie again. What was there not to feel good about?

Okay, so maybe this meeting wasn't a good sign. After all, it hadn't nearly been a full semester yet, so her probation period hadn't been served. The only change since the last meeting was the appearance of her stripper video. That didn't bode well.

"Laney, I'll cut right to it. The committee has met and concluded that you've successfully passed your probation. Furthermore, we agree that there is no reason to lengthen your tenure clock."

It was as quick as that. But Laney couldn't quite process it that quickly. What committee? Who were these mysterious people deciding her fate, a committee that didn't seem to exist in the faculty handbook? Perhaps she would get her questions answered post-tenure. The thing to focus on now was that there was still a chance at tenure.

Don't look a gift horse in the mouth.

Laney suspected the active students and perhaps a few parents had a strong voice in the matter, especially Alex and Blaine's parents.

"That's great news, Sharon. Please relay my thanks to… the committee." She did not keep the question out of her eyes. "So, I didn't have a full probationary period?"

Sharon looked out her window. "No. We were a bit too hasty with thinking that a full semester would be necessary to determine your suitability for remaining at the college."

Laney nodded, still unconvinced that nothing else had been at play. But again, why question a good outcome? "You mentioned the tenure clock, though. You don't think this probation situation knocked me off track? I can get away with keeping on track and not setting it back?"

Sharon swiveled in her chair, looking at her hands. "I don't want to guide your decision, Laney, because I don't want that responsibility on my shoulders. Everyone's case is different. But as we know, your past major reviews have been nothing short of spectacular. The real risk might be if things have gone downhill since that time."

Laney felt confident that the opposite was true. Even if her progress had plateaued, she was pretty high achieving in the first place.

"I want to take that chance. I want to remain on schedule."

"Great." Sharon put her readers back on and jotted down

some notes. "I'll document this conversation and draft an official letter regarding your tenure timeline. You'll receive official communication from the president's office confirming the decision around your probationary status."

Really? She had a clean slate? "Okay. Is that it?"

Sharon half turned to her, peering over her readers. "Unless you have more questions?"

Laney took in a deep breath. "Actually, yes. In the interest of full transparency, all cards on the table… I don't know whether you have knowledge of a particular aspect of my background that has recently come to the attention of some members of the campus community." She paused but did not discern any recognition in Sharon's gray eyes. "Specifically, I was an exotic dancer in college. It was to pay for my studies. Recently, a video of me from those days has emerged and circulated online. I'm telling you this because it may well factor into your final, final decision." There. She got it out.

Sharon nodded. "I'm aware, and I believe that Steve is aware. Frankly, I made sure that the whole committee was made aware," she responded, referring to the president and the mysterious colleagues who decided her fate. "I don't think we have much to say on that matter, although of course we'd hoped that the fallout would blow over. We've heard complaints from few parents, and only one board member expressed concern. As far as most of us are concerned, it's in your past. Long ago. We're more disturbed by whether it was a student who posted the inappropriate material online."

Laney sighed relief. Thank god. Thank god!

"So, any other questions or concerns?"

"Nope." Laney stood up and took it as a good sign that Sharon was not walking her to the door. It was business as usual this time. No grave goodbye.

"Thanks, Sharon."

"You bet," the provost called over her shoulder.

Chapter Twenty-Nine

MARCH WAS A milder month than usual. Flora were confused, and tulips could actually be spotted here and there. Birds waited for daylight savings time to begin before they began demanding that sleepers wake up and listen to their songs. Walking out the door was a generally pleasant experience, both in mild temperatures and a fresh, slightly green atmosphere.

Tie hadn't told anyone about his birthday on the twentieth although somehow HR must have let the station staff know, as they brought in a cake and put it in the kitchen, making him join them at noon so that they could sing an off-tune "Happy Birthday" to him. Not to mention Blue's excited proclamation, as she was always trying to get him to celebrate the date of his birth. He never saw the point, but just appreciated if the day brought beauty and peace.

After his show, he drove to Laney's where they decided to have their meeting. It took longer to arrange than he was hoping because of their busy schedules, but he also sensed they were both nervous.

"Still cream and sugar, I assume," Laney stated rather than asked.

Tie waited a beat. "I haven't changed that much, although I have done some soul-searching."

She paused her stirring, looked up at him, and continued.

She finally sat across from him, cups steaming. She jumped back up. "Oh, some cookies. Or toast. What would you like?"

"Nothing, really. Laney, sit down, please."

She did as she was told. "It's just so strange to have you in my house again."

Silence. Then they started at the same time.

"I'm ready when you are—"

"Tie, I don't think—"

And simultaneously, "Go ahead." And they laughed a little together.

"Seriously, I don't know where to start, because I don't know what we are anymore, what I've done to us, who you are to me." She sighed. "It's been a while for us, I guess."

He nodded, his golden-brown locks shaking. "I understand, honey."

"Especially when you look at me with those beautiful eyes," she said shyly. "I feel like I'm baring my soul."

He uncurled her fingers from her mug and placed his large tan hand on hers, massaging it with his thumb. Despite the seriousness of the situation, it felt so good to feel her soft skin again, to be in contact with the missing half of his world. Her face flushed and she shifted in her seat.

"What do you want us to be?" he asked. "Who do you want me to be to you?"

"Come on, Tie, that's not fair. You know the answers.

You shouldn't make me feel vulnerable again."

"I think it's important for you to be vulnerable with me, honey, before we can move anywhere." His lips tingled as they grew fuller. "And, by the way, it's not a cinch for me to sit here across from you and your own beautiful browns… I'm scared to death. But you're worth everything to me."

She stared into the nearly black liquid in her mug for a while. He didn't rush her. Finally, she looked up at him.

Her voice was slightly shaky. "I want us to be a couple again. Like we were. Well, not like we were because I guess we're both different now, but I do want to be romantically exclusive again. Not that I've been with anyone else," she quickly added.

He nodded and kept his eyes on hers, but didn't say anything. His heart sped up and he doubted he was keeping the excitement out of his eyes. Perhaps the effect encouraged her.

"And so, I want you to be my partner. Partner in discovering life. Sorry that sounds cheesy," she said, her cheeks reddening. "But that's really it. In a nutshell. I've missed you so much." Her eyes were shining with tears.

"It doesn't sound cheesy," he said, though laughing with immense joy. He was surprised to feel a tear fall from his eye. "It sounds like my birthday wish!"

They gazed at each other, communicating and questioning with their eyes.

"But are you sure about this, Laney? I don't think I could have my heart broken again." His eyes were watering, threatening more tears.

"And I couldn't do that to you—to us—again."

The relief nearly made him weak. He wanted to smother her with kisses and squeeze her so tightly she might scream for help. Instead, he played it cool. "You're serious? You did the ultimate mic drop and now you want to come back to the stage?"

"It wasn't a—" She reached across and playfully shoved him. "You've been reading Urban Dictionary again, haven't you? You know that's not my language, right?" She smiled.

"Seriously, though, Laney. Can you envision yourself bringing me to one of your African-American functions on campus? Can you introduce me to your Black colleagues, or the occasional family member, without trepidation?"

"Yes. God, I'm proud of what we had. It was so special. I'm serious, baby. I've even started a blog devoted to those of us in—or who have been in—multiracial and multicultural relationships. It's called Transcendent Colors because it's something I actually believe in. I had an epiphany or two." She smiled, wiping away a few tears.

He smiled. "I know. I'm one of your followers." He turned away. "It's just hard to read sometimes because you talk of us in the past tense."

"Oh, *you're* the other reader," she joked.

In actuality, she had three hundred and ten followers. Tie had noted that, for someone who hadn't liked anyone in her business, she had become surprisingly comfortable with sharing her story. "You know, the blog is devoted to you, despite it all."

He looked back at her. He wondered if the appreciation showed in his eyes. He didn't say it, but he silently dedicated at least half his radio shows to her, if only to help him make it through the show.

"So you know I'm beyond that specific racial hang-up. I've gotten past the race thing in relationships. Although, of course, I'm still racially conscious, and I'd expect you to be. I think it was all about struggling to figure out things about myself, and what I valued. I can't promise I'm over that, but I can promise that I won't run away from you because of any real fears."

Tie continued to stroke her hand. "And I can promise you that I won't harden myself to you in order to protect myself, or be so quick to think you're rejecting me. We're equals."

She cocked her head, waiting for him to elaborate. But he couldn't find the words to elaborate at the moment. And his insecurities didn't seem as crucial as they had even just a few hours earlier. Somehow, nothing besides this moment seemed crucial. As he studied her face, which had often appeared in his fantasies, he hardened in his pants.

He stood and lifted her from her seat, sat down, and put her on his lap. It felt so good to have her soft bottom against his thighs again. And near his crotch, which was straining by the second.

"I think we can do this together. I feel so much for you. If you only knew how much." He kissed her, and their kiss deepened as they finally allowed each other full access to their delicious, eager tongues. He pulled back, breathing rapidly. "Okay, but, where were we? We have a lot more to talk about, don't we?"

"Yes, but you accept me, warts and all." She slid over and stared at the obvious bulge in his crotch. "So let's do what we both want to do so that we can talk later without distraction, hmmm?"

Those were the last words exchanged between them for over two hours. Tie's thoughts weren't turned off, though, and as he followed her up the steps, watching her curvy ass, he thought about how much he missed engaging in all his senses with her. Missed the taste and texture of her mouth, and the smell, taste, and texture between her beautiful legs. Missed her modest blushing every time he started to go down on her, modesty that quickly turned into intense moans and her pressing his head more deeply into her sweet heat. Missed her soft lips and gifted tongue on him. Missed her legs wrapped around his waist as her inner walls tightly held him, aided by the fact that she was so, so wet. Missed the contrast of their skin tones as they lay gazing at each other afterward.

Of course, he didn't have much time for nostalgia as they were undressed and entangled on the bed in record time. Time to make new memories.

LANEY PADDED OUT to her kitchen, where she found Tie happily making pancakes and humming to himself.

"Hey, sunshine!" He called to her over his shoulder.

She yawned and wrapped her arms around his waist, resting her disheveled head on his muscular back. "Mmm. What are you so chipper about? Well, making up—many times—with you did, of course, make me happy too. But you seem especially excited."

"Well…" He turned around, pulled her to him and cupped her face. "I'm whipping up a nice breakfast that'll bring a smile to your face." He kissed her forehead.

Then Laney picked up on the smell of coffee and bacon. She went to pour herself a cup. "You want?" she called over her shoulder.

"Sure thing." He slid the pancakes onto two plates and placed a couple of strips of crispy-looking bacon on each. Spinning her lazy Susan, he found what he was looking for. "Truly a girl after my own heart. Real maple syrup. Not the colored corn syrup I grew up with. And blueberries on the side, which I forgot to put in the batter." He gave a sheepish grin.

She looked at the plates on the table. "Thank you so much. This is sweet." She wrapped her arms around his neck. "I admire everything about you, too, Tie Stevens. Who would have thought my soul mate would reach me through the airwaves? You're like a sexy genie who came out of my radio to grant all my wishes." She kissed him. "Because you're all I could ever want."

Chapter Thirty

THE DAY AFTER his birthday, after his workout and before he headed to the studio, Tie's cell rang. He answered, despite that it was his default ringtone, and immediately recognized the number.

"Mom?" he answered.

The man on the other line cleared his throat, a deep clearing that then led to a small fit of coughing. "You okay, Dad?" Tie tried to keep the astonishment out of his voice. Then it suddenly occurred to him. "Is *Mom* okay?"

"We're both fine!" He sounded like his cantankerous self, at least when talking with Tie.

Silence.

"Well, when are you coming back to Chicago? Your mother and sister miss you."

"Oh, did Meg tell you I moved?" He hadn't bothered to tell either of his parents. His cell number was the same; they knew how to reach him.

"She did, but not before I heard it on the radio first." His father's response was gruff.

Tie was floored. His father had heard his program? At least part of it? At least once? To what did he owe the honor?

"No big deal," was his father's grumpy follow-up.

Knowing better than to push it, he tread lightly. "I actually like Columbus, but I'll likely be broadcasting from Chicago sometime later this year."

Silence.

"Um." Tie's turn to clear his throat. "I should tell you, and you can tell Mom... you're going to be in-laws." Tie had no idea what possessed him to say that, and what to expect next, but he realized he was clutching his phone so hard that his hand was starting to cramp.

There were another few moments of silence. "In-laws, huh?" There was a note, a new one, Tie detected in his father's voice, but he couldn't place it. It was higher in pitch than his usual dour notes that was for sure. "Huh. So you're going to be a husband. I think...think you can handle that."

Tie wasn't sure how to respond. That was as close to a compliment as he'd ever received from his father, and if it had nothing to do with his academic or career achievements, so be it. This must have taken some balls on Mike Stevens's part, to admit his son might not completely fail at something.

"Who's the woman?" he demanded.

Tie smiled, despite himself. "Um, her name is Elaine Travers... she's up for tenure this fall." He despised having felt compelled to add in the academic aspect. He should not be catering to his father, dammit.

"A professor? Of what?" His father's voice belied any disinterest.

"Psychology."

"Could do worse, I suppose." He paused. "Somehow you

ended up drawn to academia, after all, huh?" There was something triumphant in his father's voice that Tie chose not to acknowledge.

"Well, she's a beautiful, brilliant woman. Just so happens she's also an academic—who is attracted to me." He figured the point would be lost on his egocentric father, but he made it nonetheless. "Anyway, if you and Mom can come, you'll certainly be invited to the wedding. We haven't set a date."

"No date! Hmmph."

It occurred to Tie that, since they could one day become grandparents, they might be interested to learn that they might have a biracial grandchild in the future. "Dad... she's Black, my fiancée. African American. You know what that means..."

A beat ensued on the other end. "That her ancestors were from Africa? That you have good taste in women? I don't know—what the hell does it mean?"

Tie tried not to laugh. "I do have good taste in women. But it also means that one day you'll have a biracial grandchild. I just don't want you to be caught off guard when you see pictures."

"I guess that indeed would have caught us by surprise," his father said, thoughtfully. "You, Tie. You're full of surprises, aren't you? Never one to follow the predictable path." His father chuckled—actually *chuckled*. Apparently Mike Stevens was the one dropping surprises today.

"Well, Tie. I don't want to take too much of your time. Oh, your mother's here—I forgot. She'd like to acknowledge your birthday."

Mike Stevens handed the phone over to his wife without saying goodbye, but that was as rewarding a phone conversation Tie could have ever hoped to have had with his dad—ever.

He sat, dazed, though his mother's predictable questions. *Is she pregnant? Did we miss the wedding? Will it be in a church? Have you called your sister?* "Oh! Happy birthday, darling!"

But when he ended the call, he somehow felt fifty pounds lighter.

TIE WAS NERVOUS. He'd spent any hour he could steal in jewelry stores, looking like a lost boy. He lucked out, finding a ring on his first expedition. He'd been incredibly presumptuous in telling his parents they were going to be in-laws. It was time to tell Laney. Well, to *ask* her. But they were in the delicate phase of early renewal of a relationship. This could be one of his moments of pushing too hard, too quickly.

He chose this restaurant, Ginger, especially for her, although under the pretense that they were celebrating his birthday. He had only casually mentioned his birthday after their pancake breakfast, and she had been horrified she hadn't known his birthday was the day before. Hence, the insistence on celebrating. There were white lilies on every table, and beautiful light blue tablecloths that looked good at any period of the day, in any lighting. He was looking forward to seeing her reaction when she arrived. The evening lighting sent striking colors through the large windows, and the lilies bathed in the vibrant sunrays. The sunset over the water would be magnificent tonight.

He saw her first, in a fabulous blue dress and with her hair styled in long romantic curls. She looked heavenly, and he couldn't wait to have her in his arms. She glanced slowly around the restaurant and a small smile crept onto her face. She walked toward him. They embraced, and it was one of the best feelings in the world, as he smelled her hair and kissed her soft cheek.

"This is beautiful, but we're not celebrating *my* birthday. This is *your* day. Well, three days after your day."

"If you could see your smile right now, you'd understand why this is just as much a gift for me." He had the urge to capture her smile on camera, these precious moments that he'd lose if he ever lost her again. But he reminded himself to stay in the moment, to be with her.

"You're quite the charmer." Her smile turned coquettish.

They ordered their drinks and stared at each other for several moments.

"You know, I heard from my father a couple of days ago. Actually, he tried to call me on my birthday but I was preoccupied." He looked out the window.

Laney gasped. "On your birthday? Is your mother okay?"

He laughed. "First thing I asked. She's fine. The old guy just called to talk to me for a moment. Get that. He said I might be an okay husband." Tie smiled again. "I mean, that's as good as it gets."

"An okay husband? How did he jump to that?" She

looked startled.

He had to face what he'd done. In his mind, they were forever bound. He saw himself and Laney happily married, but they'd never actually talked about it.

His eyes locked with hers as his face warmed. "Laney, you must know that I… I love you."

Her cheeks became tinged with pink, and her eyes started shining. He took her hand.

"And I know we've only just reconciled, but in my mind, I wanted to marry you months ago. I mean, then again maybe you're against the institution? We haven't really—"

"No, I'm not against marriage. I just haven't… let myself… but Tie"—her eyes were still shining—"that's what this has all been about, hasn't it? The heartache and the confusion, in addition to the ecstasy." She looked out the window for a moment and then looked back to him, eyes brimming with tears. "This whole… mess… it's been about love. Baby, I love you too."

He moved his chair closer to hers and they embraced and shared a tender kiss that slowly grew deeper and more probing. Until they remembered where they were.

But there it was… what Tie suspected for some time. She loved him. His Laney, full of love. Love and light.

He smiled shyly and reached under the table, fumbling with his pocket. He produced a small, deep blue velvet box and opened it for her. It was an elegant princess-cut white sapphire set in platinum with delicate scrolling. Small blue sapphires at the side complemented the sparkling center. The stones were tasteful but large enough to draw attention.

Laney knew that Tie would think twice before getting her a potentially problematic diamond.

"I'd like you to have this, anyway, because I think it would look beautiful on your dainty hand." He looked down for a minute. "But"—he met her eyes again—"I would love to make you my wife. And I'd love to be your husband. We never talked about the institution and all that, so I didn't want to do the on-one-knee thing... usually I know you so well but I was a little lost here," he said shyly. "If you would rather—"

"Yes!" Laney interrupted, tears escaping her eyes. "Of course, I want to marry you."

Tie's heart sailed as he placed the ring on her finger.

She admired the ring. "It's extraordinary!" But focused on him, her fiancé. "And you totally get me. I wouldn't want the on-one-knee thing. I like to be discreet. And I know this is sapphire! And... you should expect to be getting a ring from me soon, too."

He smiled. "Of course. We're equals. We'll share symbols of our bond now." He put his hand in his other pocket and rummaged around. "I might have a rubber band. That could suffice for now."

"Silly!" Laney laughed, covering her mouth. "I will *not* have my fiancé missing a finger on his wedding day." Her face grew thoughtful. "This is all a shock to me. I can't even think what we're supposed to do next." Her cheeks warmed. "I still have this vague princess thing in my head that I really need to act out, so I'll need to do all the silly wedding-planning stuff."

"I'll help."

"I know you will. If Nette will let you."

On cue, the sun began to send its most spectacular colors across the sky, and they took each other's hand and looked toward the horizon.

"Here you are, sir. And are you ready to order?"

"Could you just give us a few minutes, please?" Laney asked, turning from the window only to glance at Tie. As the imperial colors reflected in her eyes, he was awestruck by what he'd found.

WALKING ALONG THE Scioto by moonlight, Laney glanced at him and he was gazing at her with the most love in his eyes she'd ever witnessed.

Tie squeezed her hand. She still felt the same current and that wonderful lightness of being she experienced at his first touch. Judging from the way Tie's lips parted, he was feeling the same. This was what their love felt like, looked like, smelled like, and tasted like. Forever, this was what their love would be like.

The End

If you enjoyed this book, please leave a review at your favorite online retailer! Even if it's just a sentence or two it makes all the difference.

Thanks for reading *Degrees in Love* by Tavi Wayne!

Discover your next romance at TulePublishing.com.

TULE
PUBLISHING

If you enjoyed *Degrees in Love*, you'll love these other books from Tule's American Heart imprint!

One More Round
by Shelli Stevens

It's Complicated
by Nikki Prince

Beautiful Wreck
by Kasey Lane

Forgive Me
by Kimberley Ash

Heartthrob
by Robin Bielman

Available now at your favorite online retailer!

About the Author

Tavi Wayne is an educator and a lifelong learner. She lives outside of Philadelphia with her husband and son. She has been writing stories since she was six (under another name). She adores writing tales of romance. She also enjoys reading, good company, beaches, moon rises and sunsets, and good food.

Thank you for reading

Degrees in Love

If you enjoyed this book, you can find more from all our great authors at TulePublishing.com, or from your favorite online retailer.

TULE
PUBLISHING

CPSIA information can be obtained
at www.ICGtesting.com
Printed in the USA
FSHW020933150120
66058FS

9 781951 786137